1

For Jill: The best friend any writer could ever wish for.

CHAPTER ONE

"Smells like nothing else on earth, doesn't it?" Grant Webber said to Detective Sergeant Jason Smith.

The head of forensics walked In front of Smith down a long corridor and stopped outside a closed door.

"I'd say a week at least," Smith said.

They'd been called out to a shared student house on Jenkins Road, one of the main student hubs on the outskirts of the city of York. One of the students hadn't been seen for over a week – her room hadn't been opened in all that time and now, a foul stench was coming from inside.

"Do you want to do the honours?" Webber asked Smith.

Smith turned the spare key in the lock and took a deep breath. He grabbed the handle and opened the door.

The putrefying stench of human decay was unmistakable. Smith stepped back as the warm malodorous reek entered his nostrils. He put his hand over his mouth and nose and surveyed the room. The cause of the smell was lying on the bed. The woman was lying on her back. Her eyes were open and she had a gaping wound in her neck. Her face was a sickening greenish-grey colour and the tongue in her open mouth was swollen.

"Looks like she was stabbed in the neck," Smith observed. "I'll leave you to it – I wouldn't want to contaminate your crime scene."

"Thanks a lot," Webber said. "What do you think?"

"First impressions?"

"Of course."

"She knew her killer," Smith said. "And this is where she was killed. There's dried blood on the bed. And I'd say she didn't get on very well with her housemates."

"What makes you say that?"

"Come on, Webber," Smith said. "She hasn't been seen for over a week, and she's only reported missing when there's a stink coming from her room. I'll let you work in peace."

"Hand me that spare key," Webber said.

Smith gave it to him – Webber compared it with a similar key on a small desk against a wall.

"It's a match," the head of forensics said.

"I'll let you work in peace," Smith told him once more.

Smith stepped outside into the fresh air and lit a cigarette. The crisp February air made him shiver. He closed his eyes and tried to picture what had happened inside the house. The dead woman was Kirsty King. She was twenty years old and was in her second year of a law degree at the University. She was reported missing by Frances Walker. Miss Walker rented the room next to Kirsty's.

DS Bridge's car pulled up and Bridge and DI Brownhill got out.

"What have we got?" Brownhill asked.

"Not a pretty sight," Smith told her. "I reckon she's been dead for at least a week. Webber's in there now."

"Who called it in?"

"Housemate. Miss King hadn't been seen for over a week, but the housemate only called it in because of the stench coming from the room she rented."

"Is it that bad?" Bridge said.

"I've seen worse," Smith mused. "It looks like she was stabbed in the neck and just left on the bed."

"Where is the housemate now?" Brownhill asked.

"Inside the house. I suppose we should tell her the bad news."

Frances Walker sat in the living room with her hands around a hot mug of tea. Smith and Bridge sat down on a two-seater sofa.

"I'm afraid it's bad news," Smith told her. "Kirsty is dead. She's been dead for quite some time."

"What happened?" Frances asked matter-of-factly.

"We don't know yet. When did you last see Kirsty?"

"About a week ago."

"And you didn't think it was odd that you hadn't seen her for so long?" Bridge said.

"Not at all," Frances said. "We share a house and that's as far as it goes. We're not exactly friends, and it's not unusual for Kirsty to disappear into her room for days on end."

Smith did some quick mental arithmetic. "Let's say it was a week ago when you last saw Kirsty, can you remember how she was?"

"What do you mean?"

"Was she acting strange at all?"

"I don't think I paid her too much attention," Frances shrugged her shoulders. "Like I told you, we're not exactly friends."

"OK," Smith said. "Do you know if Kirsty had a boyfriend?"

"I don't think so. She spent so much time on her law degree she wouldn't have had time for it."

"What about friends?" Bridge said. "Do you know any of her friends?"

"I told you," Frances said. "We share a house – that's pretty much the end of it. Do you know when they're going to take the body away? That stink is making me feel ill."

"Is it just you and Kirsty who live here?" Smith asked.

"There are four of us. Janet and Gayle are away. They're both studying archaeology so they go away on digs a lot. I can't see how I can be of any help. I've got a lecture in half an hour I have to attend."

Smith realised they were wasting their time. "Thank you, Miss Walker. If you do think of anything else, please give me a call."

He handed her one of his cards.

"Oh," he'd thought of something else.

"Yes?"

"How many keys are there to Kirsty's room?"

"What?" Frances said.

"The door was locked," Smith told her. "We used a spare key to open it, and there was a matching key on the desk in Kirsty's room. Are there any more keys?"

"Not as far as I'm aware."

"Thank you, Miss Walker," Smith stood up. "We'll probably need to talk to you again."

"Will that stench ever go away?" she asked him.

Smith left the room shaking his head.

"She was a bit cold-hearted," Bridge said.

He and Smith sat on the wall outside the house. Smith took out his cigarettes and lit one.

"Her housemate has been lying dead for over a week and she didn't seem to give a monkey's." Bridge added.

"We live in a cold-hearted world," Smith said.

"This house used to belong to The Ghoul, didn't it?"

"I thought it was familiar."

Smith thought back to the time another student had been found dead in the kitchen. His good friend, The Ghoul had been the main suspect for a while.

"What are the odds on that?" Bridge said. "Two dead students found in the same house?"

"We live in a cold-hearted world," Smith said again.

Webber came out of the house. He rubbed his hands together and took a deep lungful of fresh air.

"That stench is going to linger in my nostrils for weeks," he said.

"Have you got one of those for me?"

He pointed to Smith's cigarette. Smith took out the packet and handed it to him.

"What do you think?" he asked.

"Looks like the wound to her neck was what killed her. There was something odd about the whole scene though."

"Odd?"

"There wasn't that much blood, considering that gaping wound in her neck."

"Maybe the carotid wasn't severed," Smith suggested. "We'll know more when the path guys have done their thing. Did you find anything useful?"

"I pulled a few prints," Webber said. "We'll have to wait and see what they can tell us. And there were two wine glasses in the room, so I'd say she had company before she died."

CHAPTER TWO

Landscapes don't cut it these days.

That's what the proprietor of the new art gallery on the main road had said.

Landscapes don't cut it.

What does he know?

He doesn't know what exquisite landscapes these are.

The artist stood back and inspected the latest one. It depicted a bleak vista of red soil set against a fierce blue sky. A single Bloodwood Tree formed the main focus of the painting. The whitewashed bark of the tree was surrounded by orange-red sand dotted with hardy bush.

The artist inspected the latest work from a different angle. The perspective was good but not perfect. The tree was too close – it ought to have been painted further back on the horizon. That way, the eyes would see the colour first.

The colour of the true Australian Outback.

It was the colour of death.

What does the owner of the art gallery know about true art? The artist mused.

Surely all art is about life and death – the purity of life and the beauty of death, and all that lies in between. The shades between being born and breathing out that last fetid breath.

The colours on the canvas in front of the artist were breathtaking. No other landscape was more desolate and barren than the Australian Outback, and the pigment in the paint the artist used really did do the terrain justice.

The artist removed the painting from its stand and replaced it with a blank canvas.

A new beginning.

But there was no more paint left – the nature of the paint, and its quick drying properties meant many more layers were needed than conventional paints.

The blood was finished.

The artist would need to find some more.

CHAPTER THREE

"Here we are again," Brownhill said.

The DI and the team all sat in the small conference room at the station. Smith, Bridge and DC Whitton sat in a row on one side of the table – DC Yang Chu sat next to Grant Webber opposite them.

"What do we have so far?" Brownhill looked at Webber. "Grant?"

"Not much at this stage," the head of forensics admitted. "The young woman's housemate called it in because there was a rotten stench coming out of the room. We'll get more from pathology, but I'd say she's been dead for at least a week. The heating was on in the room and it had been closed for all that time according to the housemate. I pulled some prints, but besides that I couldn't find much else. There was no sign of a struggle, nothing broken, and I didn't get the impression it was a burglary gone wrong."

"Smith," Brownhill said.

"The woman's name was Kirsty King," Smith began. "Twenty years old. She was in the second year of a law degree. As far as we know she kept herself to herself. No boyfriend and very few friends."

"Another one," Bridge chipped in.

"Bridge?" Brownhill said.

"Why do murder victims always seem to have no friends? Most of the murders we've investigated involved real losers."

"Easy pickings," Smith said. "There was something odd about the scene, though. Actually, two things. The woman's throat had been slashed open and yet there was very little blood."

"Maybe she was killed somewhere else," Yang Chu suggested.

"And then taken back to her room, placed on the bed and left there with the door locked?" Smith said. "I don't buy it, and that brings me to my second point. The door to the room was locked. The housemate told us there are only two keys. Kirsty's key was found on the desk inside her room and the other one we used to open the door."

"Which means the killer used the spare to lock the door behind him," Whitton said.

"Exactly."

"Unless there's another key somewhere," Yang Chu joined in. "Maybe the killer had a copy. Has the landlord been contacted? Maybe the landlord has spare keys to the place."

"We'll speak with the landlord later today," Smith said.

"What's your suggested plan of action?" Brownhill asked Smith.

"Same as usual," Smith replied. "Motive. Who would want to kill a young law student?"

"Do we know what she was killed with?" Whitton asked and Smith frowned at her.

"Have you not been listening?" he said. "We didn't find anything else at the crime scene, and the path blokes have barely started."

"What are your initial thoughts?" Whitton articulated each syllable with such venom that everybody in the room turned to stare at her.

"Probably a knife," Webber interjected. "Very sharp and possibly with a serrated blade. As Smith said, we'll have more to go on when the initial path report comes in."

"Right," Smith said. "Whitton, you and Bridge can speak to the landlord. PC Baldwin has his contact details. I want to go to the hospital and speed up Kenny Bean and his team. Once we know more about how she died we may get a bit closer to why she died. Yang Chu, you're coming with me."

"Is everything alright with you and Whitton?" Yang Chu asked as Smith drove far too quickly out of the car park at the station.

"Fine," Smith mumbled. "Not that it's any of your business."

Yang Chu took that as a hint not to ask any more questions and they drove in silence the rest of the way to the hospital.

Things were far from fine between Smith and his wife. There had been a tension between them for a while now – a tension that neither of them seemed to be able to work through and it was slowly reaching boiling point. Neither of them really knew exactly how or when it had all started – it was sometime after Christmas, but they both knew something had to be done. They couldn't go on like this. It was only going to end badly.

Smith parked outside the entrance to the hospital and he and Yang Chu got out of the car. The wind had picked up from the east and icy gusts cut into their faces as they quickly made their way inside. Smith marched past reception and down the corridor towards Dr Kenny Bean's office. Yang Chu had to run to keep up. The young DC was used to Smith's temper – he'd been at the sharp end of it on more than one occasion, but this was something entirely different and he didn't like what appeared to be brewing in his DS's head.

Dr Kenny Bean was not in his office. Smith realised he was probably still busy with Kirsty King. He had insisted on Kenny making it a priority.

"Can I help you?" a woman Smith recognised approached them.

"We're looking for Dr Bean," Smith told her.

"He's busy with the woman who was brought in this morning. He should be almost finished with the prelim."

"Do I know you?" Smith asked her.

"Dr Dessai," she held out a hand. "I was temporarily in charge of pathology before Dr Bean came here. I've moved on to greater things now. We've met a few times before."

"Dr Dessai," Smith shook her hand. It was surprisingly warm. "Of course. My memory isn't as sharp as it used to be. Is it okay if we wait for Kenny in his office?"

"It's not my place to say. I'd better be going."

Smith thought it an odd thing to say but he said nothing. He watched as she walked down the corridor.

Dr Kenny Bean arrived ten minutes later. Smith was sitting behind his desk typing something on his phone when he walked in.

"Have you decided on a change of career?" Kenny asked.

Smith looked up from his mobile phone. "Not likely. I wanted to know if you've got anything for us yet."

"That thing you have in your hand is a wonderful invention," Dr Bean said. "As is the computer you're sitting in front of. Why do you always have to visit me in person? I am capable of sending an email or making a phone call. And could I have my desk back please?"

"Sorry," Smith stood up. "Where did you get that chair? It's much more comfortable than the one in my office. What have you got?"

Dr Bean sighed and glanced at Yang Chu. "I don't know how you can possibly work alongside that man and not go insane."

"He has his moments," Yang Chu said.

"You're not squeamish, are you?"

"Not at all," Yang Chu replied.

"Then come with me. I have something interesting I want to show you."

"We bumped into the lovely Doctor Dessai," Smith told Dr Bean as they walked. "I forgot she used to head up the department."

"A long story," Dr Bean said. "And one I'd prefer not to dig up. Here we are."

He opened up the double wooden doors that Smith knew led to the mortuary and a wave of icy air hit them in the face. Four metal tables stood against the far wall. Kirsty King was lying on the one closest to the door. Her blue feet stuck out from underneath a white cotton sheet.

"This is all very interesting," Dr Bean said and approached the table. "If not a tad disturbing."

Smith and Yang Chu walked up and stood behind him. Yang Chu flinched when Dr Bean removed the sheet. He hadn't been at the crime scene and this was the first time he's seen Kirsty King's bluish-black corpse. Her eyes were closed, and her tongue no longer protruded from her black lips, but the gash in her neck was now wide open.

"We haven't quite finished with her," Dr Bean began. "And I still have to confirm a few things, but I can tell you there was no sign of sexual assault. What do *you* think killed her?"

He directed the question at Smith.

"The wound to her neck?" Smith speculated.

"That's what I first assumed. It's deep and the carotid artery has been severed."

"But?"

"And it's a huge but," Dr Bean turned around and smiled.

"Go on," Smith urged.

"The incision in her neck was clean. Surgical, even, and a wound such as this would drain her blood in seconds. That is if she had any blood left in her to drain."

"What are you saying?" Smith was finding all of this hard to digest.

"There was very little blood left in her. That's what I'm saying. Whoever did this somehow took every last drop of her blood before slicing her throat."

CHAPTER FOUR

"Someone drained her blood?" DI Brownhill exclaimed.

The team were gathered once more in the small conference room.

"That's the conclusion Kenny Bean came to," Smith said. "And I've never known him to make a mistake before."

"No," Brownhill agreed. "Dr Bean doesn't make mistakes."

"He found needle marks on her arm," Smith continued. "It appears the poor woman's blood was removed and then her throat was slashed to make it look like that's how she was killed."

"Do we know for certain she didn't die from the laceration to her neck?" Bridge asked.

"One hundred percent," Smith said. "That's why there was hardly any blood at the scene. You've seen the result of a severed carotid artery – the blood spurts out all over the place. No, Kirsty King only had a few drops of blood left inside her when her throat was cut, and she was certainly dead way before then."

"Do we know how long she's been dead?" Bridge said.

"Five or six days."

"Bloody hell," Yang Chu said.

"Why?" Brownhill asked the next question. "Why would someone drain a body of blood?"

"And why slice her throat open if she was already dead?" Yang Chu said.

"And how did they do it?" Whitton joined in. "I've given blood and it took about ten minutes just to donate one unit. How much blood do we actually have inside us?"

"It depends on the size of the person," Smith said. "But roughly five litres. Ten units."

"So that would take close to two hours," Yang Chu did the maths. "I can't believe someone would somehow gain access to her room, and then spend almost two hours draining her of blood."

"I think she was drugged," Smith said. "Mercifully, I don't believe she actually knew what was going on. Dr Bean will have a tox report for us before the end of the day."

The room fell silent for a moment. Everybody in the team appeared to be trying to process this macabre information.

"What did you get from the landlord?" Smith finally broke the silence.

"Bugger all," Bridge said. "He claims he only has a key for the front door of the house – there are spare keys for each of the rooms, but they're always kept inside the house."

"Then whoever did this knew about the spare keys to the rooms," Smith said. "Kirsty King's key was inside her room, the door was locked, so unless she suddenly came back to life and locked the door from the inside, the door was locked with the same key we used to gain entrance this morning."

"Did Webber check the key for prints?" Bridge said.

"First thing he did," Smith replied. "Nothing."

"We need to find out who has access to those keys," Brownhill said.

"This is quite disgusting," Yang Chu said. "Why would someone drain every last drop of blood from a young woman?"

"A blood transfusion?" Whitton said. "It wasn't that long ago; people were having their organs removed remember? Or have you forgotten about almost becoming heartless?" She glared at Smith. "Maybe someone needed an urgent blood transfusion and they couldn't go to a hospital to get it."

"I don't think that's it," Smith said.

"Of course you don't."

"We'll know more when the tox reports come in, but I'm almost certain she was drugged, and if that's the case whatever drug was used will be in her blood and therefore it'll probably be useless for a transfusion."

"And you're suddenly an expert?" Whitton scoffed.

"I'm only relating what Dr Bean told me. It looks like you haven't had enough coffee today."

"That's enough," it was Brownhill. "This isn't helping. We have somewhere to start at least. Smith, I want you and Whitton to go back and speak to Kirsty King's housemate."

"I've already spoken to her, boss," Smith said. "She doesn't know anything, and I'd rather take Yang Chu with me."

"This is not open for debate. Bridge, you and Yang Chu can get over to the University. Speak to Kirsty's fellow students and lecturers. Somebody must know something about this woman."

"It's Friday afternoon, Ma'am," Bridge reminded her. "If my days at Uni are anything to go by, most of the students and probably all of the lecturers will be in the pub by now."

"Just do it. If she's been dead for five or six days, it means she was killed sometime last weekend. Ask around. Someone might have seen something."

"Are you not speaking to me now?" Whitton asked Smith as they headed towards the outskirts of the city.

"What are you talking about?"

"You've hardly said a word to me for days."

"That's not true," Smith said even though he knew it was.

"I don't even know who you are most of the time."

"Can we talk about this later?" Smith asked.

"It's always later isn't it? You never want to talk about anything when I ask you."

"We're working, Erica," he said and realised he'd spat out her name. "This isn't the time. We'll talk later. I promise."

They walked up the short path to the house on Jenkins Road and Smith rang the bell. The door was opened a short time later by Frances Walker. From the scowl on her face it was obvious she wasn't pleased to see them. She glared at Smith and looked Whitton up and down.

"Miss Walker," Smith said and smiled. "We need to ask you a few more questions. Can we come in?"

"Do I have a choice?"

"It would be better for you to talk to us now," Smith told her. "Now, can we come inside? It's Baltic out here."

They sat in the living room. The smell of Kirsty King's putrefying body was still apparent, although it wasn't nearly as pungent as before.

"I told you everything this morning," Frances immediately assumed a defensive stance. "There's nothing more to tell you."

"Miss Walker," Whitton said. "We believe Miss King was killed sometime last weekend. Can you remember what she was doing last weekend?"

"I already told him," Frances looked at Whitton. "Kirsty and I hardly spoke. I didn't pay her much attention."

"And yet you share a house?" Whitton said. "Isn't that a bit odd?"

"I signed the lease in September last year," Frances told her. "Myself, Janet, Gayle and Lisa. We've been friends since Fresher's Week."

"Janet and Gayle are the archaeologists?" Smith said.

"That's right."

"And who is Lisa?"

"She doesn't live here anymore. She was studying accounting, but she got offered such a good job in London she couldn't see the point in carrying on at Uni, so she dropped out."

"So, where does Kirsty come into the equation?" Whitton asked.

"When Lisa left, her room became available. We didn't even want anybody else here – we pay the same rent on our rooms however many people are living here, but the greedy-bastard landlord advertised it and Kirsty moved in. She's been here since November, and I've probably said more words to you today than I have to her in three months. I can't help you with anything."

"Where were you last weekend?" Smith decided on a change of tack.

"I was probably at my boyfriends."

"Probably?" Whitton said.

"I was," Frances said. "Why are you asking me where I was? You can't possibly think I had anything to do with this?"

"And Janet and Gayle?" Smith ignored the question. "Were they around?"

"They've been at the dig since mid-January. Crazy if you ask me. Who on earth goes up to the Shetlands in January?"

"You were at your boyfriend's?" Smith said. "All weekend?"

"I often go there when Janet and Gayle are away," Frances said. "I don't really like being alone in the house."

"But Kirsty was here," Whitton pointed out.

"You know what I mean."

"We'll need your boyfriend's contact details," Smith said.

"He has nothing to do with any of this," Frances said. "Neither do I."

"Miss Walker," Whitton said. "A young woman has been killed. You share a house with this woman, so it's natural we will want to ask questions."

"I told you – I can't help you."

"Come on, Whitton," Smith stood up. "Let's go."

CHAPTER FIVE

Bridge and Yang Chu were having slightly more luck at the University. Bridge's earlier assumption that students and lecturers alike would be propping up bars at this time on a Friday afternoon was proven to be correct, but it appeared that York University's Faculty of Law were slightly more conscientious than their colleagues in some of the other departments. A young, chubby woman with thick glasses directed them to the faculty head's office, and Bridge knocked on the door. It was opened by a large man with a friendly smile.

"Good afternoon," Bridge took out his ID. "DS Bridge and this is DC Yang Chu. Could we please have a word?"

"Of course, come inside, and please forgive the mess. This is what we teachers of lawyers call our Friday chaos. Dr Henry Dewbury at your service, but please call me Henry."

They went inside, and Bridge could see straight away what Henry was talking about. Stacks of papers littered all three of the desks in the room – more papers were piled on the chairs around the desks, and flip-files lay open on the floor.

"Please take a seat," Henry cleared two of the chairs for them and sat down behind his desk. "What can I do for you?"

"I'm afraid one of your students was found dead this morning," Bridge came straight out with it. "Kirsty King."

Henry's smile disappeared. "Kirsty? Dead?"

"We're afraid so. That's why we're here. We're trying to find out more about her – who her friends were, that kind of thing."

"I can't believe she's dead. What happened?"

"We can't go into that right now," Bridge said. "Did you know her well?"

"She was top of her class in her first year," Henry said. "And I could see no reason why she wouldn't repeat that this year. My God, this is just awful."

"Doctor Dewbury," Bridge said. "Sorry, Henry, I have to ask this, but we believe Kirsty has been dead for quite some time – almost a week, so didn't you think it odd that she hasn't been seen in classes all week?"

"Not at all," Henry replied. "The law faculty here at York prides itself on an innovative and forward-thinking approach, to quote the University's brochure, and unlike years ago, a large chunk of the work involved can be done off-campus. We actually encourage our scholars to problem solve away from the University. Kirsty often spent long periods of time working at home."

"We're trying to retrace her movements from last weekend," Yang Chu said. "Her housemate was away, so we were hoping you could help us."

"Help you?"

"With some names of friends and acquaintances," Bridge elaborated.

"Of course."

Henry got up from his desk and left the room. He returned a few minutes later with the chubby woman who had ushered them in earlier. The woman had tears running down her face. She sat down on the windowsill, removed her glasses and rubbed her eyes.

"This is Petra," Henry said. "She knew Kirsty well."

"Petra," Bridge said in a gentle voice. "I know this is hard, but we need to ask you a few questions. Will that be okay?"

She nodded.

"You knew Kirsty King? Is that correct?"

Another nod.

"Do you know if she had a boyfriend?"

"Nobody special," Petra spoke for the first time. "She didn't have time, what with the undergraduate degree, but there is this bloke she spent a bit of time with."

"Is he also doing a law degree?" Yang Chu asked.

Petra shook her head again. "He's studying art history I think."

"Art history?" Bridge repeated. "Do you have a name for us?"

"Greg something," she started to cry again.

"Take your time," Henry said.

"Greg Walsh," Petra sobbed. "His name's Greg Walsh."

* * *

"If he's doing an art degree, he'll definitely be in the pub on a Friday afternoon," Bridge said to Yang Chu as they walked along the aptly-named Yellow Brick Road back to where they'd parked the car.

"You shouldn't be so hasty to attach stereotypes," Yang Chu said.

Bridge stopped walking and looked at his colleague like he'd just grown another head. "Did you just hear what came out of your mouth? You sounded just like a bloody student."

"Just because he's an art student doesn't mean he spends most of his time getting rat-arsed."

"Ten quid," Bridge said.

"What?"

"Ten quid says we'll find him in the nearest, cheapest student pub."

"You're on," Yang Chu said. "Be prepared to part with your money."

The interior of the Young Trout was nothing like its name suggested. There was nothing inside the student drinking hole to explain why it was called the Young Trout. Bridge felt instantly out of place. He felt old. The clientele here were mostly in their late teens and early twenties. Bridge scanned the room and the melancholy that had washed over him when he'd entered the pub immediately disappeared as he took out the photograph he'd been given by a member of the art department at the University. The man sitting alone in the corner of the room was definitely the same man in the photograph, and Yang Chu was going to leave the Young Trout ten pounds worse off.

"Greg Walsh?" Bridge said to the man at the table.

He looked up at Bridge and squinted behind his small round-rimmed glasses as though his eyes had suddenly been blinded by bright light. "That's me. Do I know you?"

Greg Walsh looked to be in his early thirties. His ponytail and John Lennon glasses suggested he was a career student. Bridge looked around the room. It was still early afternoon, so the pub wasn't that busy yet.

"Police," he said. "Can we have a word?"

This information appeared to have no effect on Greg. "Take a seat. What can I help you with?"

"We need to talk to you about a woman by the name of Kirsty King," Bridge said.

"Go on."

"She's dead, Mr Walsh," Yang Chu told him.

"Dead? There must be some kind of a mistake."

"I'm afraid not," Bridge said. "When did you last see Miss King?"

Greg appeared to be thinking hard. He stroked his goatee beard with his forefinger and thumb.

"Just over a week ago, I think," he said eventually.

"And you didn't think it was odd that you hadn't seen your girlfriend for so long?" Yang Chu said.

"Kirsty isn't my girlfriend – we are just friends, and it's not unusual for her to disappear into her own academic world and be consumed by her degree. How did she die?"

"We're not sure yet," Bridge told him.

"But you think it's suspicious, otherwise you wouldn't be here asking questions."

"I believe you're studying for an art degree," Bridge changed the subject.

"Art History," Greg elaborated. "You could say I collect art degrees. This is my third."

"So, you don't work then?" Bridge said.

"I'm in the fortunate position of being able to study for as long as I like," Greg took a sip of his beer and closed his eyes. "I was left a lot of money when my parents died. I have no family, but I'm able to fund my passion. I still can't believe Kirsty is dead. We used to have long chats about all kinds of things."

"You said you last saw Kirsty around a week ago," Bridge reminded him. "Can you remember exactly when it was?"

"Sometime over the weekend. Yes, we had coffee on Saturday afternoon."

"And she seemed fine to you?"

"The same as usual. Chatty and excited about the new semester. We spoke for a couple of hours and went our separate ways."

"That's all for now, Mr Walsh," Bridge said. "Thank you for your time. We will need to speak to you again."

"I'm always around."

Bridge and Yang Chu stood up to leave. Yang Chu turned around.

"What sort of art are you into?"

"I'm going through a bit of an experimental stage right now," Greg told him. "A Vincent Castiglia/Francis Bacon kind of vibe."

CHAPTER SIX

"What sort of question was that?" Bridge asked Yang Chu as they made their way back to the station. "*What sort of art are you into*?"

"Just curious, that's all," Yang Chu replied. "I used to be quite good at art at school. I've never heard of that Frank Bacon bloke though. What did you make of Greg Walsh?"

"There was something odd about him."

"Besides being a career student?"

"The woman we spoke to at the law department at the University seemed to think Kirsty spent a lot of time with the man and yet he hadn't seen her for a week."

"Do you think he killed her?" Yang Chu asked.

"He's a suspect and we'll bring him up at the next briefing. Hopefully Smith and Whitton have got something out of that housemate."

"Do you get the impression that all's not well in the Smith household?" Yang Chu said.

"No, and it's none of my business anyway."

"There's tension between them – I can feel it."

"It's nothing to do with us. They'll sort whatever it is out in their own time."

* * *

"Are you trying to get us both killed?" Whitton screamed.

Smith had just overtaken a slow-moving truck.

"There was loads of room," he said. "I missed the car coming the other way by miles. Do *you* want to drive?"

"At least then we'd get there in one piece."

Smith took a deep breath and screeched to a halt on a double yellow line. "Right. You want to talk. Talk."

"What's happening to us?" Whitton said. "Since Christmas we've barely said two words to each other."

"That's not true," Smith said. "We talk."

"Barely. We get home from work, sort Laura out and you disappear into your own little world. And you're drinking more than you used to."

"I am not. I've always had a drink after work. It's never bothered you before."

"That's not all. You've turned into a different person since that venom thing. I don't even know who you are anymore."

"Stop saying that, Erica," Smith said, much louder than he intended. "I am the same bloke you married. That thing with the venom really woke me up. Our daughter could have been killed."

"But she wasn't."

"It made me see things differently, that's all. And it made me do a lot of thinking."

"About what?" Whitton asked. "About us?"

"Of course not. About me. About what I'm doing with my life, and how it's affecting the people I love. I don't know if I want to do this anymore, Erica. When what I do every day puts the people I care about most in the world in harm's way it makes me question whether it's really worth it."

"Why didn't you tell me all this before?" Whitton's tone had softened slightly.

"Because I knew you'd try and talk me out of it. You always do."

"I love you, Jason Smith," Whitton said. "But you are your own worst enemy. You over-analyse things to the point where it becomes obsessive. And you are probably the best detective York has ever seen."

"Probably?"

Whitton slapped him on the shoulder. "Now, can we please stop moping and go and do what they pay us to do?"

Smith smiled and pulled away from the kerb.

Bridge was chatting to DC Baldwin by the front desk when Smith and Whitton came in. Bridge had a huge grin on his face.

"What's up with you?" Smith asked him. "Did you win the lottery or something?"

"Better than that," Bridge told him. "Baldwin has agreed to go out on a date with me."

"We're going for a drink," Baldwin corrected him. "It's not a date."

"Don't do it," Smith warned her. "Relationships at work never pan out."

He walked off down the corridor leaving Bridge, Baldwin and Whitton wondering if they'd just heard him correctly.

Brownhill and DCI Chalmers were sitting together in the canteen. Smith got some coffee from the machine and joined them.

"You look like you need that," Chalmers pointed to the coffee.

"You're not wrong there, boss," Smith said and took a sip. "We didn't get anything useful from Kirsty King's housemate – she was with her boyfriend all last weekend. We still need to check it out, but I get the feeling she was telling the truth. It looks like Kirsty was alone in the house all weekend."

"We've got the tox reports back from Dr Bean," Brownhill said. "What blood Kirsty had left inside her came up positive for Flunitrazepam."

"Rohypnol?" Smith said.

"She was definitely drugged," Brownhill said.

"We need to find how it got into her system."

"There were small traces of the drug in the dregs at the bottom of one of the wine glasses found in her room. The other glass didn't give us anything. No prints, no DNA, nothing. It looks like it was wiped clean."

"So, that's how she was drugged," Smith said. "At least we can confirm now that she definitely knew her killer."

"Have you spoken to her boyfriend?" Chalmers asked.

"We've just come from talking to him," Bridge had come in. Whitton and Yang Chu were with him.

"And it looks like they weren't boyfriend and girlfriend," Bridge continued. "They were just good friends. He said the last time he saw Kirsty was last Saturday. They spent a couple of hours over coffee and went their separate ways."

"She died on Saturday or Sunday," Smith said. "Her friend was possibly the last person to see her alive. What did you make of him?"

"He seemed harmless to me," Bridge said.

"Career student," Yang Chu added. "His parents left him a load of cash, so he's planning on staying a student for the rest of his life."

"What a sad life," Smith said. "Anything else?"

"There was something a bit odd about him," Bridge said.

"Go on."

"I can't quite put my finger on it."

"We'll bring him in. Dr Bean found traces of Rohypnol in Kirsty King's system, so we can assume she was drugged before her blood was removed. Which would suggest..."

"She knew her killer," Whitton repeated her husband's earlier words.

"And she was drugged inside her room – I can't see someone drugging her and dragging her lifeless body inside, can you?"

"No, I can't," Smith agreed. "Go and find this friend of Kirsty's."

"Greg Walsh," Yang Chu said.

"Greg Walsh," Smith repeated. "Go and find him and tell him his presence is required here right now."

"Smith," Chalmers said. "Have you checked your emails recently?" Smith realised he hadn't had a look for a few days. "I've been busy, boss. Is there something I should know about?"

"Superintendent Smyth has been away on a course in The Hague," Chalmers said. "But he'll be back on Monday. You do realise what time of year it is."

"Shit," Smith said. "Old Smyth is going to put us through another of his mind-boggling crime stats presentations, isn't he?"

"I'm afraid so. I thought with the course coinciding with the end of January we might get away with it this year, but it looks like the old fool isn't such an old fool after all."

Superintendent Jeremy Smyth's annual crime stats presentations were legendary for all the wrong reasons. Years ago, Smyth had got it into his head that a detailed statistical analysis of the previous year's crime figures would encourage the York Police to work harder to reduce the figures the following year. It didn't work. The most it succeeded in doing was to make the bungling ex-public-school Superintendent more and more of a laughing stock every year. Everybody in the employ of York Police was expected to attend. No excuses.

"I think I might be off sick that day, boss," Smith said. "It's the day after my birthday and I've got a feeling a sore head is on the cards."

"You'll be there," the DCI ordered. "And Smyth has a trick up his sleeve this year. You didn't hear this from me but the idiot has asked some representatives of the press to attend. He thought it might be good for public relations."

"I can feel that hangover coming on already," Smith stood up and left the canteen.

CHAPTER SEVEN

The artist scraped the thin film off the surface, dabbed a thumb into the new *paint* and pressed the digit onto a blank piece of white paper. The tincture on the page quickened the heart. It was even better than the artist remembered. A new landscape was already forming. With shaking hands, the artist spread the remaining *paint* out in a silver tray and gazed at the blank canvas. The canvas was ready to be brought to life – with shades of brown rarely seen. And maybe texture this time.

With eyes closed, the artist breathed deeply until the shaking subsided. The scent of the paint was exquisite – it had an almost narcotic effect on the body. The wet tip of the brush was dipped into the reddish-brown liquid and the artist was ready to begin.

This canvas was much larger than the others. This one was to be a bold endeavour.   With a steady hand, the artist sprinkled some fine flour onto a portion of the *paint*. This was carefully mixed, and the result was a thick, lumpy substance. The brush soaked up the mixture and was applied to the canvas in quick, well-practiced strokes. Again and again the procedure was repeated until an unusual red escarpment filled the background. This was topped with a fierce sunset. The artist would need to wait for the *paint* to dry before a solitary black windmill would be added in the foreground. Then many more layers would be necessary to prevent the delicate *paint* from peeling.

But there wasn't enough blood left. It was time to get some more.

CHAPTER EIGHT

"Interview with Greg Walsh commenced 17:15" Smith said. "Present DS Smith and DS Bridge."

Greg Walsh sat opposite the two DS's in Interview room 2.

"Mr Walsh has declined the offer of legal representation. Mr Walsh, do you know why you're here?"

"It's about Kirsty," Greg replied.

"Kirsty King?"

"That's right. I didn't kill her."

"OK," Smith said. "You were good friends with Miss King, is that correct?"

"We were friends. We used to have a few drinks every now and then, but we weren't that close."

"When was the last time you saw Miss King?"

"Last Saturday afternoon. I already told him that." He nodded to Bridge.

"What time was this?" Smith asked.

"We met at a coffee shop around the corner from the Minster at about noon and stayed there until around two."

"Do you know where she went afterwards?" Bridge asked.

"Home I assume. She said she had some project she needed to work on. Kirsty took her studies very seriously."

"And you haven't seen or heard from her since?" Smith said.

"No. We said our goodbyes and that was that."

"What did *you* do after you left the coffee shop?" Bridge said.

"I went for a beer at the Trout. Coffee isn't exactly my drink of choice."

"Were you alone?" Smith said.

"I bumped into a few people I know. Why are you asking me all this? I had nothing to do with what happened to Kirsty."

Smith decided to steer the interview in another direction. "Have you heard of the drug, Flunitrazepam, Mr Walsh?"

"Can't say I have."

"What about Rohypnol?" Bridge said.

"Of course, it's the date-rape drug. I'm a student – we've all been warned about it. Not leaving your drink unattended and all that. It's not just a female thing – blokes have been victims too. What are you saying? Was Kirsty raped?"

"No," Smith said. "I believe you've been at the University for quite some time."

"I like it," Greg said. "I like the whole lifestyle."

"And you're an art student. Is that correct?"

"I'm reading History of Art. I find it fascinating."

"You mentioned earlier something about an experimental stage," Bridge said. "Frank Bacon?"

"Francis Bacon," Greg corrected him. "Among a few others. Vincent Castiglia is another. True art is boundless, and these men have pushed the boundaries much further than most, and I find that very exciting."

"I'm not too clued up on art," Smith admitted. "What do you mean when you say *pushed the boundaries*?"

"They are totally unconventional," Greg was clearly becoming animated. "From subject matter and perspective to colours and materials, they experimented with something totally new."

"Do you paint?" Bridge asked him.

"Of course. I'm no Castiglia, and I'm definitely nowhere near Bacon, but I do alright."

"What kind of things do you paint?"

"I go through stages," Greg replied. "Depending on what mood I'm in. Right now, I'm really into landscapes. But in a few months, I could be equally obsessed with still life. What has all this got to do with Kirsty?"

"Probably nothing," Smith said and realised he was running out of questions to ask.

"Do you live in town?" was all he could think of.

"I've got a small two-bedroom place on Hill Drive. It's all I need. I use the spare room as a kind of studio. I really don't know how I can help you with this. Kirsty was alive and well the last time I saw her."

"Interview with Greg Walsh concluded 17:30," Smith said and switched off the machine. "Thank you for your time, Mr Walsh. If you think of anything else, please contact us."

"What do you think?" Bridge asked when Greg Walsh had left the room.

"He's not our killer," Smith replied. "I don't like him – I can't stand students and I can't imagine why anyone would want to stay a student for so long, but he's not our man."

"I still think there's something weird about him."

"He's an artist. They're all a bit weird."

"What now then?"

"It's getting late. And I promised Whitton I'd take her out for a meal tonight."

"Are you and her alright?" Bridge asked. "You seem to have been arguing a lot lately."

"That's what married people do. You'll find that out one day when you become a grown up."

"Not likely. I've got plenty of single years in me yet. And I've got a date with the lovely PC Baldwin to look forward to tomorrow."

"It's not a date," Smith reminded him.

"We'll see. I'll see you bright and early in the morning. Enjoy the meal out."

CHAPTER NINE

"Don't you worry about this little lady," Harold Whitton told Smith. "She knows how to make herself at home here. It's Friday night – go out and enjoy yourselves."

"Thanks, Dad," Whitton said. "Are you sure it's no trouble?"

"Don't be daft, love," her mother, Jane said. "You know we love having her. Are you going somewhere nice?"

"There's this new Indian place on the Foss Road, and I'm looking forward to the hottest curry they've got."

"You'd better get going then," Harold said. "And don't think you have to rush back – we'll have Laura for the night."

"Your parents are brilliant," Smith told Whitton as the taxi pulled away from their house. "I don't know what we'd do without them."

"Where to, boss?" the taxi driver asked from the front seat.

"India Delight," Smith told him. "It's on the Foss Road."

"I know it. I took the wife there last week. Great food. Stay away from the Vindaloo, though, unless you want to redecorate your toilet bowl tomorrow."

"What a colourful thought," Smith said. "Thanks for the advice."

"Do I know you?" the taxi driver asked.

Smith sighed – he wasn't particularly keen on over-talkative drivers. "I don't think so."

"You're that detective," the taxi driver clearly had no intention of keeping quiet. "You were in all the papers."

"You must be mistaking me for someone else," Smith said. "I get that a lot. I have one of those faces."

He was glad when he'd paid the driver and the taxi pulled away from the restaurant.

"You're famous," Whitton grinned. "People will be asking for autographs next."

Smith opened the door for her. "I'm ordering you the Vindaloo. I want to see if that chatty taxi driver was right."

The restaurant was busy and there were only a few empty tables. A waiter appeared and showed them to a table for two. Smith ordered two beers and asked for a couple of menus.

"What are you going to have?" Whitton asked him. "Something mild and boring I suppose?"

"That's me in a nutshell," Smith grinned. "Mild and boring. And famous in case you've forgotten. But you're right – I'm going to play it safe and have a Korma."

"This is nice," Whitton said and finished what was left in her glass.

"It's Theakstons," Smith said. "Of course it's nice."

"Not the beer, you dope – this. Just the two of us eating out at a restaurant. I can't remember the last time we did this."

"Before Christmas I think," Smith said and sighed. "Anyway, what's on the agenda this evening? What do you want to talk about?"

"Not work. Definitely not work. Do you think we'll be okay?"

"We'll always be okay, Mrs Smith and besides, I think you're the only woman on the planet who could put up with me."

"Mrs Smith," Whitton repeated. "It does have a certain ring to it doesn't it?"

"Don't tell me you're going to ask to be called DC Smith at work?"

"I've been thinking about it. Anyway, we'd decided on no shop talk tonight. York Police Force does not exist for at least a few hours."

"We'll see," Smith mused.

The waiter appeared with two plates of steaming curry and rice. Poppadoms and various Sambols were arranged on the table around them.

"Can I get you anything else?" he asked.

"Just two more beers, thanks," Smith replied.

They tucked in. Whitton finished first. Beads of sweat had formed on her forehead and temples and she wiped them away with a napkin.

"That was a hot one," she said. "I need another beer just to take the burn away."

"I'm going for a pee," Smith told her. "I'll organise two more beers while I'm at it."

He stood up and headed for the Gents. When he'd finished, he ordered two more beers and was about to return to the table when he spotted somebody across the room. It was somebody very familiar. The woman was sitting on her own at a table laid out for two. She had short black hair and a very pale face. Smith walked over to her.

"Jessica Blakemore," he said.

She looked up at him. "Jason Smith. We meet again."

"When did they let you out?"

"I was kicked out," she told him. "They insisted there was nothing wrong with me."

Jessica Blakemore had been resident in a psychiatric hospital for longer than Smith could remember. She'd suffered a breakdown six or seven years earlier, was admitted and never showed any desire to get back into the outside world.

"It appears I abused the facility's hospitality for too long," she told him. "So now I'm back outside with the real lunatics."

"You're looking well."

"Liar. I look like death. I need some sun on my face."

"What are you doing with yourself?" Smith asked.

"I landed a gig at the University. I'm still a qualified psychiatrist but I'm more on the teaching side than the head-cracking side now. What about you? Are you still harassing murderers?"

"Of course. I'd better get back to my wife. She'll be wondering where I am. It was great to see you again. We must catch up some time."

"I don't think so. You always seem to bring trouble with you."

"Who were you talking to?" Whitton asked when Smith finally sat down again.

There were two beers on the table. Whitton had almost finished hers.

"You'll never guess. It was Jessica Blakemore."

"The nut-job?"

"She's not a nut job," Smith said. "She's just a bit misunderstood. Anyway, she's not in the mental hospital anymore – she's working at the University teaching psychiatry."

"God help the students."

"She's not that bad," Smith defended her. "Besides, she's helped me out plenty of times in the past."

This was certainly true. Many times, over the past few years Smith had turned to Jessica for advice, not only on work problems but with personal issues too.

"Well I'd stay away from her if I were you."

"Is that a threat?" Smith tried to sound serious but the smile on his face gave him away. "Are you jealous?"

"Of a raving lunatic? You must be joking."

"I like it when you get jealous. It's quite sweet."

"I am not jealous," Whitton insisted as Smith's mobile phone started to ring.

"I'm going to ignore that," he told his wife. "For once I'm going to ignore a phone call."

The ringing ceased but almost immediately Whitton's phone blasted out a loud Meatloaf introduction.

"You really need to change your ringtone," Smith told her.

"It could be my parents," Whitton said, took out the phone and sighed. "It's the switchboard at work. I suppose I should see what it's all about."

She pressed *answer*. "Whitton."

Smith watched as her facial expression changed from deep concentration to what could only be described as utter disbelief. The conversation was very one-sided, but Whitton joined in every now and then with an, *I see* or an, *Okay*.

"What's happened?" Smith asked when she'd finished the call.

"There's been another murder," Whitton told him. "Not that far from here as it happens. A student was found in the alleyway that runs along the back of the Foss Road. Webber is on his way there with the DI."

"They can deal with it then," Smith said. "They don't have to drag us away from a night out."

"There's more. The man who found the body mentioned something disturbing. He's a third-year medical student apparently, and he tried to see if there was anything he could do to help. He reckons the young woman's body looks like it's been drained of blood."

CHAPTER TEN

The alleyway where the young girl was found ran along the back of the White Rabbit pub, a drinking hole mostly frequented by students on weekends as they offered various specials on alcohol. A crowd of people had gathered at the front of the pub. It was still reasonably early but from the sound of some of the voices, Smith could tell that they'd been enjoying the cheap alcohol for a good few hours. For once, Smith had arrived on the scene before Grant Webber. The head of forensics appeared a couple of minutes later accompanied by DI Brownhill.

"You got here quick," Webber commented when he approached.

"Me and Whitton were enjoying a meal out at an Indian place just down the road," Smith told him. "And you know me, always on duty."

"Do we know what we're looking at?"

"I haven't seen the body yet. Apparently, the bloke who found her is a medical student and he reckons she's had her blood drained out of her."

"Another one?" Webber shook his head. "What the hell is happening in this town? Where is she?"

"Round the back in the alley. The uniform who answered the call is keeping people away from the body. Let's see what we've got shall we?"

They walked around the pub and turned onto the narrow access road that ran the whole length of the Foss Road. An icy wind blew straight through the narrow alley. Two PC's were standing next to a large skip looking at something on the ground. One of them turned around when he heard Smith and Webber's footsteps and shone his torch directly into Smith's eyes.

"Turn that bloody thing off, Constable," Smith said. "Or at least shine it somewhere else."

"Sorry, sir," the PC said.

Smith knew him to be PC Allen Fish, and he was relatively new to the job. He didn't recognise the other man.

"Has she been moved at all?" Webber asked Fish.

"No, sir," the young PC replied. "Not by us anyway. The man who called it in said he tried to see if he could help her, so he might have touched her."

"Where is he?" Smith asked.

"Who, sir?"

"Who do you think? The bloke who found her. Where is he now?"

"He went back inside the pub when we got here. He didn't seem too upset, considering."

"He's probably seen worse," Webber said. "He is a medical student."

Smith leaned over the woman on the floor to get a closer look. "Hand me that torch," he said to PC Fish.

Smith shone it on the woman's face and gasped. The light from the torch was far from flattering, but this woman was as white as snow. Her pale-blue eyes were open. The shade of red lipstick she had chosen to wear lent her whole face a ghostly appearance. The garish red contrasted greatly with her pallor. Smith shone the torch beam up and down her body. She was wearing a pair of jeans and a white T-Shirt.

"Not exactly appropriate clothing for this time of year," he thought out loud.

The woman's arms were the same colour as her face.

Smith switched off the torch and handed it back to PC Fish. Two of Webber's forensics officers arrived.

"I'll leave you to it," Smith said to Webber. "I can't see any initial signs of injury, but there are spots of blood on her T-Shirt. I'm going to have a chat with the bloke who found her. What does he look like?" He addressed this question to PC Fish.

"You can't miss him, sir. Big and fat. And he's wearing a jumper with the Wombles on the front. His name is Snowdon. Seth Snowdon."

"I want you both outside the entrance of the pub," Smith told him. "Nobody is to go in or out until I say so."

"Right you are, sir." Fish said.

Smith was glad to get inside the pub. The February winds had chilled his whole body. Whitton and Brownhill were sitting at a table with two women. They both appeared to be in their early twenties, and they were both wiping tears from their faces. Smith scanned the bar. Seth Snowdon was nowhere to be seen. The door of the pub opened, and Smith turned around. It was DS Bridge.

"I was just up the road," Bridge told him.

"You and me both," Smith said. "It appears that half the York Police were out and about a stone's throw from where a murder victim turned up. What are the odds on that happening?"

"I would have preferred to stay where I was. I was making some real progress with a woman I met in a pub round the corner."

"I thought you and Baldwin were going on a date tomorrow."

"It's not a date, remember," Bridge said. "Besides, you know me. I like to keep my options open. What do we know so far?"

"Not much. The woman was found out back in an alley. Webber and his team are out there now."

"Do you think it's connected to the other one? The other dead student?"

"I've got a terrible feeling that it is," Smith said. "And if I'm right, God knows what we're dealing with."

Smith walked over to where Whitton and Brownhill were sitting. The two women they were talking to seemed less agitated now.

"Boss," Smith nodded to Brownhill.

"DS Smith," the DI said. "These two ladies are friends of the victim."

"I'm very sorry," Smith said to both of them.

"Her name is Taylor Fox," Brownhill continued. "Second year business studies student. Miss Hill and Miss Lewis here haven't seen Taylor since Wednesday."

"So, she wasn't with you in here tonight?" Smith asked.

"We don't usually come in here," the thinner of the two said. "We just thought we'd give it a try tonight."

She spoke with a Welsh accent.

"Miss?" Smith said.

"Shelley Hill. We're doing the same course as Taylor."

"And you say you haven't seen her for two days? Is that quite normal? What about classes?"

"Taylor didn't show up at Uni yesterday," the other woman said. "Nor today. I just thought she was ill."

Smith realised two things at the same time. Firstly, he knew instinctively that the woman wasn't killed outside the pub that evening, and therefore, interviewing everybody in the White Rabbit tonight would be a total waste of time and energy.

Grant Webber appeared behind him. "Can I have a word?"

Smith followed him towards a quiet spot by the bar.

"I don't think questioning anyone in here tonight is going to help," Webber said.

"I was thinking the same thing," Smith agreed. "She wasn't killed outside the pub tonight, was she?"

"She most definitely wasn't. I'd say she's been dead for a couple of days already."

"She was last seen on Wednesday, so you could be right. Did you find anything else?"

"My guys are still at it, but as you said this isn't our murder scene, so unless we get something from the body, I don't think what we find here is going to help us much."

"What about tyre marks?"

"Nothing yet. What are you thinking?"

"I'll have to confirm it," Smith said. "But I think she was dumped outside very recently. She was found next to the skip where the empties from the pub are binned. And I'm pretty sure that the bar staff take out the empties more than once a night. Whoever left her here didn't even try to hide the body. And she was brought here by car. She had to be."

"I'm inclined to agree."

"With what?"

"With everything you just said."

"You know what, Webber?" Smith said and patted him on the shoulder. "What?"

"Shacking up with Bryony Brownhill has done you the world of good – you're not half the arsehole you used to be."

Smith walked back to Whitton before Webber had a chance to digest what he'd just heard.

"Brownhill told us to call it a night," Whitton told him. "We've got a list of Taylor Fox's friends, but that can wait until tomorrow. And the medical student who found her has agreed to come into the station first thing to make a statement. You and Webber seem to be getting on better these days."

"I knew he'd come round to my way of thinking sooner or later. Do you feel like a drink?"

"I do actually. My parents have taken Laura off our hands for the night so let's make the most of it. Not here though."

"Definitely not," Smith agreed. "I've got a feeling we're going to be sick of the sight of students before this is all over. Let's go somewhere the know-all little bastards don't know about."

CHAPTER ELEVEN

"Damn and blast!"

The artist looked the new canvas up and down.

"Damn and blast. Hell, and damnation. Damn and fucking BLAST!"

With the last word spoken, the artist shoved a foot through the painting, the canvas was ripped off the easel and thrown against the wall with such force a vase on the shelf jumped up and smashed on the floor. Somebody screamed something in the house next door, but the artist couldn't hear what they'd shouted.

"Useless."

The artist had been too eager – too impatient and the result was a disaster. There hadn't been enough *paint* – an inferior substitute had been used, and, what was now a mangled mess on the floor against the wall was not what it should be. The next one would need to be better. Much, much better.

"Tomorrow. Tomorrow we will start again. Tomorrow we will do things right."

CHAPTER TWELVE

The Hog's Head was much quieter than the pubs and wine bars in the city centre. It was much warmer too. Smith glanced across the room and scowled when he realised their usual table by the log fire in the corner was occupied by an old man reading a newspaper. A half-full pint sat on the table in front of him and Smith knew from experience that Yorkshire pensioners could quite easily nurse half a pint of beer for the whole night. Marge, the owner of the pub was filling up optics behind the bar when they approached. She beamed from ear to ear when she spotted them.

"Jason," she exclaimed. "And Erica. It's so lovely to see you again. Where have you been hiding? Pint?"

"Three please, Marge," Smith replied to her second question.

Whitton looked at him curiously. "Three?"

Smith didn't offer an explanation. He walked off towards the table in the corner.

"Bloody awful weather," he said to the old man reading the newspaper.

"Aye," the man said without even looking up from his newspaper.

"There's a fresh pint waiting for you at the bar," Smith continued. "If you'll do me a favour."

He had the man's full attention now. "I'm listening."

"You see that woman at the bar there? The one standing in front of your pint?"

"Aye," he was clearly a man of few words.

"This is where we first met. At this very table in fact, and I thought it might be romantic if I asked her to marry me at the table where it all started."

"Free pint you say?"

"It's waiting at the bar for you," Smith told him.

The old man stood up, downed his beer, picked up his newspaper and turned to Smith.

"Good luck, lad. You're going to need it."

"What did you say to him?" Whitton asked when they were sat next to the fire.

"What do you mean?" Smith said.

"The old man. What did you say to him that made him give up his table?"

"You don't want to know. This is more like it. I must be getting old. What do you make of these two murders?"

"I thought we'd agreed not to talk about work."

"Aren't you even a little bit intrigued?" Smith said. "Two young women are killed. Both were students at the University, and both had no blood left in them. They have to be connected somehow."

Whitton sighed. "You can't help yourself, can you?"

"No. And I'm certain the fact they were drained of blood is the significant part here. That's what we need to look at."

Whitton took a long drink of beer. "OK, since you're determined to go on about this, why was their blood drained?"

"What would someone do with eight pints of blood?" Smith answered her question with one of his own. "I can't think of anything to gain by extracting so much blood. I doubt you could sell it – there is no logical reason why someone would do such a thing, so now it's got me thinking about something else."

"Which is?"

"What if these women are actually connected in some way? What if something links them together? The killer could be aiming to send a message, and that's why he takes their blood after he kills them."

"I think that beer has gone to your head."

"Speak of the devil," Smith looked at his empty glass and stood up. "I'll get us a couple of refills."

He returned a short while later with two more Theakstons. He'd also refilled the glass of the old man at the bar.

"Where were we?" he said and sat down.

"The killer is sending a message," Whitton reminded him.

"We need to look closely at the victims. We know that their blood was drained from them. Something about the two of them has to tell us why?"

"We can go through all that tomorrow," Whitton suggested.

"Or maybe it has something to do with some kind of ritual," Smith wasn't finished yet. "The blood was taken for use in that ritual."

"Stranger things have happened." Whitton humoured him.

"Yes," Smith was suddenly animated. He picked up his beer and drank half of the glass in one go. "They have. Do you remember that investigation we had a few years back? The Selene Lupei case? The killer slit the throats of men by the light of the full moon. Ritualistic stuff."

"I remember," Whitton said. "I also remember your nut-job, Jessica Blakemore confessing to the murders."

"That's it," Smith exclaimed. "Jessica Blakemore."

"Are you suggesting she has something to do with this? I suppose it is quite a coincidence that she came out of the loony bin the same time these murders started. And she works at the University. Both victims were students there."

"Don't be ridiculous, Whitton," Smith said. "She's not our killer. But she can help us get inside the head of whoever did this."

"What is it with you and her? You look up to her like she's some kind of miracle-worker. She's a bona fide mental case."

"And that's exactly why she's proven to be so useful in the past, Whitton. Don't you see? Her mind works differently to most people's."

"Can we please talk about something else now?" Whitton's tone indicated that it wasn't a question.

"OK," Smith conceded. "I'm going for a pee. And when I get back, we can discuss a new ringtone for your mobile phone. Meatloaf's *Bat out of Hell* really is quite embarrassing."

CHAPTER THIRTEEN

The last customer had only just left the Green Man on Pike Street, and Rene Downs was dog-tired. Her nine-hour shift at the pub was almost over – she still had to secure the day's takings in the safe and switch off most of the lights, but then she would be finished until Sunday. She planned to spend the whole of the next day either in bed or on the sofa watching DVDs. She had a rare Saturday off, and she was definitely going to make the most of it. The weather forecasters had predicted more freezing conditions ahead and Rene did not intend on stepping outside her flat until she had to get up for work on Sunday.

She closed the door of the electronic safe and locked the cupboard it was hidden in.

"You're off tomorrow, aren't you?" John, the landlord said.

"That's right. I'm back in on Sunday for the morning shift. I haven't had a Saturday off since before Christmas."

"Get yourself off," John said. "I'll finish off here. Have you organised a taxi?"

"I only live around the corner, John," Rene told her boss for the umpteenth time.

"I know, but you shouldn't be walking home on your own at night. I can escort you home if you like."

"Thanks, but I'll be fine. See you on Sunday morning."

The icy wind bit into her face as soon as Rene opened the door of the pub. She zipped up her coat and bowed her head to shelter from the gusts. Her flat was a five-minute walk from the Green Man. If she took the short cut along the alley that ran the whole length of Foss Road, she could make it in two.

"What the hell," she said as a gust nearly knocked her off her feet.

She turned into the alley and quickened her pace. The access road was dark, but Rene knew the way off by heart. She'd often walked this route, albeit mostly during daylight hours.

As she walked Rene was sure she could footsteps behind her. Heavy footsteps.

She carried on walking. Her flat was only a couple of hundred metres away now. All she had to do was reach the next road, turn right and the building where she lived would be right there. The footsteps were still behind her, but they sounded much closer now. Rene turned into the road and headed for her flat. She stopped at the door, took out her key and opened the door.

"Sorry to bother you," she heard a voice behind her.

The owner of the footsteps, Rene thought and froze.

She turned around and sighed. "Oh, it's you."

"I left my keys in a pub down on Judd Street. I'm on my way back to get them, but I'm dying for the toilet. Would you mind if I used yours? I really need to go, and I don't fancy peeing in the alley in this wind."

"Of course," Rene said, relieved. "Come up."

She led the way up the stairs to her flat, opened the door and they both went inside.

"First door on the right," Rene said.

"Thanks."

"What's in the bag?" Rene pointed to a large holdall her visitor was carrying.

"Oh, just the bare essentials."

Rene turned around and a few seconds later she was aware of a slight burning sensation at the back of her thigh. Immediately, numbness spread from the initial area of the burn, up her leg and into her chest. Her legs gave way and she collapsed on the floor. She tried to call out but her vocal chords didn't appear to be working. She crawled forward a few feet and came to rest by a pair of black boots.

"This won't hurt a bit."

Those were the last few words Rene Downs ever heard.

CHAPTER FOURTEEN

The atmosphere in the small conference room was as cold as the streets outside the station. Smith, Whitton, Bridge and Yang Chu were gathered around the table waiting for DI Brownhill to arrive. All of them were bleary-eyed and appeared worn out. All of them looked like they could use a few more hours sleep.

Smith stretched his arms and yawned. "Where's Brownhill?"

"Running late," Bridge told him. "Car troubles. Problems with the battery again."

"Why doesn't she get rid of that old banger?" Yang Chu said.

DI Brownhill drove an old Citroen. It never stopped giving her trouble, but she was very attached to it and reluctant to trade it in.

"What's the story with the dead woman?" Yang Chu asked.

The young DC was the only one of them who wasn't called out to the scene the previous night.

"It looks like she was drained of blood," Smith told him. "We were lucky that it was a medical student who found her and he's certain she had no more blood left in her."

"Another one?" Yang Chu exclaimed. "What the hell is going on here?"

The door opened and DI Brownhill walked in. Grant Webber was with her.

"Sorry for the delay," Brownhill said. "I think it's high time I invested in a new car. Let's make a start shall we?"

She sat down at the head of the table. "The body of Taylor Fox was found outside the White Rabbit pub last night. The man who discovered the body is a third-year medical student at the University. He is positive her body had no more blood left in it."

"Medical student?" Yang Chu said. "Is he a suspect?"

"He will be in shortly to make a statement," Brownhill said. "But we are not treating him as a suspect at this moment. We'll wait to see what he has to say. The woman was a student at the University, and that fact together with the draining of the blood is what we're going to concentrate on. Smith, do you have anything you'd like to suggest?"

Smith stretched his arms again. "I do actually. Two women are killed and are subsequently drained of blood. That would suggest a killer with a rather sick mind, wouldn't you agree?"

He looked at the weary faces around the table. Nobody said a word.

"I'll take that as a yes then. I happened to bump into an old friend last night. Somebody who has proved invaluable in the past. Someone who is an expert in the field of depraved minds. I suggest we bring Jessica Blakemore in, in an advisory capacity."

"Absolutely not," Brownhill said without thinking.

"Why not, boss?" Smith said. "She can help us get inside the head of this maniac."

"She's not far off being a maniac herself," Bridge chipped in.

"She's better now," Smith insisted.

"In case you've forgotten," Brownhill added. "Jessica and I were good friends at one time. She is not the right person to help with this investigation."

"But I think..."

"No," Brownhill cut him short. "This matter is not up for discussion."

The room was eerily silent for a few moments.

"We didn't get much from where Miss Fox was discovered," Grant Webber spoke first. "But I didn't expect to. The skip outside the White Rabbit was not where she was killed. I'm certain of that. DS Smith and I agree she was brought there in a vehicle and dumped sometime last night."

"We spoke with the owner of the pub and the empties are taken out every few hours and whoever took them out would have noticed the body if it was there earlier."

"Do we know anything about the woman?" Yang Chu asked.

"Taylor Fox," Smith said. "She's a second-year business studies student. According to two friends who are on the same course, she hasn't been seen since Wednesday. She failed to turn up for classes on Thursday and Friday. So, we know she was killed between Wednesday afternoon and last night."

"My guess is she's been dead for at least two days," Webber added.

"Sometime Wednesday evening then?" Brownhill deduced.

"Looks like it."

"The path report is going to take some time, so in the meantime we need to speak with Miss Fox's friends. Did she have a boyfriend? We need to see if we can pinpoint her whereabouts from when she finished at University on Wednesday afternoon until the time she was killed."

PC Baldwin came in the room. "Sorry to interrupt, but there's a very nervous Seth Snowden waiting at the front desk. He said he was told to come in and make a statement."

"Thank you, Baldwin," Brownhill said. "We're just about to finish up here anyway. Tell him someone will be with him shortly."

"Will do, Ma'am."

"Let's wrap it up then," Brownhill said. "Smith, I want you and Whitton to find out about Taylor Fox's friends and acquaintances. The two women we spoke to last night hadn't seen her since Wednesday afternoon – they gave us her address, so speak with her housemates. They may be able to enlighten us on Miss Fox's whereabouts on Wednesday after she finished her classes. Bridge, you and Yang Chu can interview our nervous medical student. So far he's our only witness."

CHAPTER FIFTEEN

"Where are you going?" Whitton asked Smith as he turned right onto the road that led out of the city. "The address we were given for Taylor Fox is in the other direction."

"Slight detour," her husband told her. "I just want to make sure of something before we speak to Taylor Fox's housemates. Kenny Bean ought to have some indication of her time of death by now, and I know Kenny much prefers speaking face to face."

Whitton sighed. "You're impossible. He won't appreciate you just turning up unannounced you know."

"He's used to it," Smith said and shivered. "I don't think the heater on my car is working properly. Are you warm enough?"

"I'm fine. There's nothing wrong with the heater – you just tend to feel the cold a bit more as you get older."

"There's definitely something wrong with this heater, and I am not old."

"Speaking of old age," Whitton said with a grin on her face. "What do you feel like doing for your birthday?"

"Is it my birthday?"

"On Monday, you dope. If I'm not mistaken, you'll be another year closer to the big four zero."

"I'll be thirty-six," Smith corrected her. "And that is not old."

"What do you feel like doing, anyway?"

"I hadn't really given it any thought. I've never really made much of a big deal out of my birthday before. You know me – I'm a real grump when it comes to stuff like that."

"You're not a grump," Whitton said. "You're just getting old."

The woman behind the reception desk in the pathology department at the hospital smiled when Smith and Whitton approached.

"Is Dr Bean around?" Smith asked her.

"He's in his office. Shall I tell him you're here?"

"Better not," Smith said. "We'll just go straight through."

"How's the leg?"

"It'll be better when this weather warms up a bit. Thank you."

They set off down the corridor towards Dr Bean's office and stopped outside. Smith was about to knock when he heard something from inside the room. It was the sound of raised voices. He recognised one of them as belonging to Kenny Bean but the other one was unfamiliar. The argument stopped, and a few seconds later the door was opened, and a woman came out. It was Dr Dessai, the previous Head of Pathology. She glared at Smith and hurried off down the corridor.

Smith and Whitton went inside the office.

"That sounded rather unpleasant," Smith stated the obvious.

"Don't ask," Dr Bean said. "What do you want?"

"Sorry to barge in unannounced," Smith began. "But I need to ask you about a TOD for the young woman who was brought in last night."

"When do you ever make a prior arrangement to see me? I anticipated as much, and the initial examination would indicate she'd been dead for roughly forty-eight hours when I examined her this morning. Give or take a few hours. You see, we have to take into account how long she was lying there in that alleyway. The bitter cold last night will have slowed down the decomposition process somewhat."

"So," Smith thought hard. "Forty-eight hours, maybe longer. That puts it sometime between Wednesday night and early Thursday morning?"

"He's especially sharp this morning," Dr Bean said to Whitton.

"He's getting wiser in his old age," Whitton said.

"That narrows things down a bit," Smith ignored them both. "Thanks, Kenny. We'll leave you in peace for a bit."

"I'll believe that when I see it."

"What was all that about earlier?" Smith said. "With you and Dr Dessai? Does she want her old job back?"

"Not likely. Like I said, don't ask. It's a very long, tedious story and I really don't feel like discussing it now."

"No worries. See you soon." Smith turned around to leave then turned back to face Dr Bean. "What are you doing on Monday?"

"I never can tell," the pathologist mused. "It all depends on what's thrown in my direction. Why do you ask?"

"Because my lovely wife is throwing me a birthday party."

"I am?" This was clearly news to Whitton.

"Why not?" Smith said. "And as I don't have many friends, I'd like you to join me? What do you say, Doc?"

"I'd say that's probably the worst invitation I've ever had. I'll see what I can do. Goodbye, detective."

"So, I'm throwing you a birthday bash, am I?" Whitton said as they drove back towards the spires of the Minster in the distance.

"You were the one who asked me what I feel like doing," Smith reminded her. "We can have something at home. Just a few close friends. Chalmers, Bridge and Yang Chu. Maybe even the DI and Webber."

"And Dr Bean," Whitton said. "We'll never fit them all in the house. Why don't we organise something at the Hog's Head? It ought to be quiet there on a Monday, and you know how much Marge would love it."

"Sounds like a plan," Smith agreed. "We'll invite your parents too in that case, and Marge is always happy to see Laura. Hog's Head it is then. What's that address again?"

CHAPTER SIXTEEN

Bridge led Seth Snowden inside Interview room 2. Yang Chu followed behind them.

"Please take a seat," Bridge said to the chubby medical student. Seth Snowden was certainly somebody who would stand out in a crowd. He was at least six-feet-four and fat with it. His hair was thin on top and long at the back, and the large glasses he wore made his face seem almost owl-like. He was wearing a huge woollen jumper with a badly embroidered image of one of the Blue Meanies from the Beatle's film, *Yellow Submarine* on the front, and a peculiar odour seemed to hover in the air around him. Bridge turned on the recording device.

"Mr Snowden," Bridge began. "This is not a formal interview – we just need to ask you a few questions about what happened last night outside the White Rabbit pub in town."

"I thought I was here to make a statement," Seth said. "Why is this being recorded?"

"To save time, ours and yours, we need to ask you a few things. Did you know the woman you found next to the skip? Taylor Fox?"

"I seem to recall seeing her around campus, but we weren't friends."

"You're a medical student," Yang Chu said. "Is that right?"

"Third year. It's hard work, but I'm enjoying it."

"Do you know what you're going to specialise in?"

"What's that got to do with the woman I found?"

"OK," Bridge said. "You found Miss Fox next to the skip outside the White Rabbit pub on Foss Road. Is that correct?"

"You already know this."

"For the record."

"I found her lying there. At first, I just thought she'd passed out. She'd had too much to drink, but when I took a closer look, I knew straight away that she was dead."

"What time was this?" Yang Chu asked.

"I can't say for certain, but it was around nine. Maybe nine-thirty."

"What did you do then?" Bridge said.

"I tried to see if I could do anything," Seth said. "I've got medical training. I turned her so her airways would be open."

"Mr Snowden," Bridge said. "You just told us you knew she was dead. And yet you tried to help her."

"I'm training to be a doctor. I had to try something, but when I felt how cold she was and when I saw the colour of her skin, I knew it was hopeless."

"What were you doing outside in the alley, Mr Snowden?" Yang Chu asked. "If I remember right, it was freezing last night. What were you doing out there?"

Seth's face reddened slightly. "This is all a bit embarrassing, but I was having a piss."

"Were the Gent's in the pub out of order?" Bridge said.

"They were full, and I really needed to go. I know the place well – I used to work there, so I went out the back."

"And did you see or hear anything?" Bridge said. "While you were outside relieving yourself."

"Nothing," Seth replied. "I finished off and that's when I saw her. She was so cold. And her face had no blood left in it. I could see that straight away."

He bowed his head and started to sniff.

"Thank you, Mr Snowden," Bridge decided they'd got enough out of him. "That will be all. If you do happen to think of anything else, please get in touch."

* * *

Smith stopped his car outside the address they'd been given for Taylor Fox and he and Whitton got out. The wind had died down slightly, but it was still bitterly cold.

"This is a bit upmarket for a student pad," Whitton commented. "When I was a student, we had to make do with a shared place in one of the shadier parts of town."

The house was a detached double storey affair in a quiet neighbourhood some distance from the town centre.

"It's quite a walk to the University from here," Smith said. "I wonder why she chose this area. Let's see if we can find out anything from the people she shared a house with, shall we."

They walked up the cobbled driveway towards the house and Smith knocked on the door. It was opened shortly afterwards by an elderly woman with sparkling-blue eyes. Smith's initial thought was they had been given the wrong address – this intelligent-looking woman definitely didn't look like a student.

"Sorry to bother you," he said. "I'm Detective Sergeant Smith and this is my colleague, DC Whitton. We were led to believe that a student from the University lived here. Taylor Fox?"

"Taylor?" the old lady said. "That's right. She rents a room in my house. Lovely girl. What's this all about?"

"Could we come in please, Ma'am?" Whitton asked.

"Of course. And less of this Ma'am business. My name is Kimberley Leith, but please call me Kim."

They were led down a wide hallway to an immaculate living room. Smith was no expert on interior design, but he reckoned the fittings and furnishings had to be very expensive.

"Would you like some tea?" Kim asked them. "Or coffee? It's coffee that detectives usually drink isn't it? I read a lot of mystery books, you know. Since my William left me, I've got all the time in the world to read. He's been gone three years now."

"Coffee would be great, Mrs Leith," Smith said.

"Give me a minute. I'll bring the works."

She returned a few minutes later with a pot of coffee, a jug of milk and sugar in a bowl. "Help yourselves, please."

Smith poured himself and Whitton some coffee and sat back down.

"Mrs Leith, I'm afraid we've got some bad news. Taylor Fox was found outside one of the pubs in the town centre last night. She's dead."

"I see."

It wasn't the response Smith was expecting.

"Do you understand what I said?" he said.

"Of course. What happened?"

"That's what we're trying to find out," Whitton said. "How long have you known Taylor, Mrs Leith?"

"Please, call me Kim. She's been living here eighteen months or so. Such a lovely girl. One of those with her head screwed on. She was really serious about her studies – that's why she opted for a room away from the hustle and bustle of the student scene. What a damn shame. Do you think she was murdered?"

"It looks like it," Smith said and Whitton stared at him with wide eyes.

"When was the last time you saw Taylor?" he asked.

"That would be Wednesday morning," Kim said. "My memory is still very much intact. She headed off for classes the same time as usual."

"Mrs Leith," Whitton said. "Sorry, Kim, today's Saturday. Didn't you think it odd that Taylor didn't come home on Wednesday? Nor Thursday or yesterday for that matter?"

"Taylor rents a room here and that's as far as it goes. I have to respect her privacy. If she wants to tell me about her life, that's fine, but I don't pry. Besides, I've been at my sister's in Harrogate since Thursday morning. I only got back this morning."

"Sorry, Kim," Smith said. "We didn't mean to sound rude, but we have to ask these questions. Would it be possible for us to have a look at Miss Fox's room?"

"Of course. If you go up the stairs, it's the first door on the right. Taylor never locks it."

Smith and Whitton walked up the stairs. The door to Taylor Fox's room was wide open. Inside, the room was spotless. There was a large map of Wales on the wall opposite the door, but the other walls were bare."

"This definitely doesn't look like a student room," Whitton commented. "The bed's made – you could probably bounce a coin on it and look at the bookshelf. All the books are neatly stored. There are no posters of the latest pop stars or film promos on the walls, and not a speck of dust. Are you sure she was a student?"

"Times must have changed since your sordid time at University, Whitton," Smith said.

He approached a desk with a laptop computer on it. He opened it up and switched it on. "Password protected. I wonder if there's anything on here that can give us any ideas about what happened to her."

"It's a long shot," Whitton said. "But we can get Webber to go over it. He's got this new IT whiz on his team, and he can get into any computer."

There was a small cupboard next to the bed. Smith opened it up but all it contained was a few dog-eared paperbacks.

"I was hoping to find some kind of diary. I don't think we're going to find anything," he said to Whitton. "Grab that laptop. I think we're about done here."

"OK," Smith said when they came back downstairs. "Kim, can you remember whether Taylor said anything about her plans for Wednesday? After her classes were finished?"

"She did mention something about a meeting with the head of one of the other faculties."

"Please go on."

"Taylor was reading business studies," Kim said. "But I seem to recall her mentioning something about the degree not being challenging enough, so she decided to add another couple of modules. Business law was one of them. And psychology if I'm not mistaken. She planned to meet somebody in the law department to discuss something. I can't tell you what I'm afraid."

"That's fine," Smith said. "Do you remember who she was meeting? Did she mention a name?"

"I'm afraid not. Like I said, I don't like to pry. Are you going to catch them?"

"Sorry?"

"Are you going to catch whoever did this?"

"Yes," Smith said without a moment's hesitation. "Yes, we're going to catch them."

CHAPTER SEVENTEEN

"She reminded me of my Gran," Whitton said as they drove back towards the town centre. "She had all her marbles right up until the day she died."

"Did you notice her reaction when she found out that her lodger was dead?" Smith asked. "That was probably the coolest I've ever known someone to be when they're told that somebody they know is dead."

"I suppose the older you get; the less death fazes you."

"Wise words. I thought I was supposed to be the old wise one."

"It's true," Whitton said. "I was surprised at you blurting out that we believe Taylor Fox was murdered. Aren't we supposed to keep that kind of info quiet until we're absolutely certain?"

"Are we not certain?"

"Of course we are, but you know what it's like, with the press these days."

"I hardly think Mrs Leith rushed to the phone and called the York Herald as soon as we drove off."

"I suppose you're right. We didn't get much out of her anyway."

"Didn't we? Kirsty King, the first victim was studying law. Taylor Fox had a meeting with someone in the law department who may have been one of the last people to see her alive. Do you see a pattern somewhere?"

"You can't possibly think someone in the law department is involved in this?" Whitton said. "Are you saying there's a future lawyer out there who just happens to have a thirst for blood?"

"You know my feelings about lawyers, Whitton. We need to check it out anyway."

"There will be nobody there on a Saturday."

"Then we'll find out where they live. Bridge and Yang Chu spoke with the head of the department yesterday – we'll get all the details we need from him."

"I still think you're barking up the wrong tree with the law faculty."

"Taylor Fox finished classes on Wednesday afternoon," Smith said. "She had a meeting scheduled with someone in the law department afterwards. A few hours later she is killed. It needs checking out. I'll run it by Brownhill, but the DI will agree with me."

* * *

"Smith," Brownhill began. "Let's run through what we've got so far."

The team had gathered once more in the small conference room. It was getting late, and Bridge didn't look too happy about still being at work. He glanced at his watch and frowned.

"With respect, Ma'am," he said. "We all know exactly what we've got. Bugger all. We're all knackered, and I don't think we're going to come up with anything new today. Can't we go through everything tomorrow morning?"

"No we can't, Detective Sergeant. Smith."

"Right," Smith looked across at Bridge and shook his head. "The first victim was Kirsty King. Twenty-year-old law student. She was found in her room on Thursday after her housemate complained about the smell. She'd already been dead for three or four days by then. She had very few friends – no boyfriend we're aware of, and she was a conscientious student. Evidence at the scene suggests she knew her killer – her door was locked, and the key was found inside the room. The only spare key was on a set that only the people who live at the house have access to. It has been confirmed that Kirsty was alone in the house during last weekend. Traces of Rohypnol were found in her system. Traces of the same drug were found inside one of the wine glasses in her room. The other wine glass was clean, so it's pretty clear she was drugged before her blood was removed."

"Taylor Fox," Smith continued. "Found beside a skip behind one of the pubs in town. She was also a student at the University, and she also had her blood removed. She was last seen on Wednesday afternoon, and all indications are she was killed shortly after that. Whitton and I have just come from the house where she rented a room, Webber's going over her laptop to see if there's anything on there that might give us some new ideas, and the old lady she lodged with gave us some new information that needs checking."

"New information?" Brownhill sat up straighter in her chair.

"Apparently Taylor Fox was due to attend a meeting with someone after classes on Wednesday. Somebody in the law department. Whether or not that meeting took place is, we don't know yet, but we need to find out who that meeting was scheduled with. With the initial path report and the information we gathered from some of Taylor's fellow students, there is such a small window of time involved between the last time she was seen until the time she died, that whoever she was due to meet is vital to this investigation."

"I agree," Brownhill said. "Get onto it."

"Now?" Bridge didn't even try to hide his disgust. "It's after six on a Saturday, and there will be nobody at the University. It can wait until Monday morning."

"No, it can't," Smith said, louder than usual. "Time is of the essence. I don't believe our killer has finished."

"The brilliant DS Jason Smith's sixth sense again?" Bridge scoffed.

"Yes." Smith looked him directly in the eyes. "These two murders were carried out by the same killer and there is no reason to think he will stop at two. Get hold of that Doctor of Law you spoke to yesterday and get the contact details of everyone in his department."

"Have you forgotten I hold the same rank as you now?" Bridge wasn't giving up.

"Then start acting like it."

"Get those details," Brownhill ordered.

CHAPTER EIGHTEEN

Henry Dewbury had been more than happy to speak to Smith when they'd spoken on the phone thirty minutes earlier. The head of York University's law faculty had informed Smith he would be at home all evening. Dr Dewbury's house wasn't what Smith had expected a Doctor of Law to live in. It was a modest two-up, two-down semi-detached property just outside the town centre. Dr Dewbury was taking something out of his car when Smith arrived.

"DS Smith, I assume?" he shouted in a friendly tone. "I'm just unpacking the rest of the groceries. Go inside. I'll be two ticks."

Smith made himself comfortable on a leather armchair in the living room. Paintings of all sizes adorned each of the four walls. Most of them were landscapes. The colours in them were very unusual. Brownish-red dirt formed the foregrounds and the backgrounds were mostly painted with a lighter, but similar tint.

"Those are the more bearable ones," Dr Dewbury came in the room. "You wouldn't believe how many canvasses I've torn up over the years."

"Did you paint all these?" Smith asked.

"Every last one. They're not masterpieces, but I like them. Can I offer you something to drink? I'm having a beer myself, but I suppose you don't like to drink on duty."

"It's never stopped me before. Beer would be great."

While Dr Dewbury was fetching the beers, Smith stood up and took a closer look at the paintings. He was no art critic, but he could see that some of them were really very good. There was something unique about them – he wasn't sure if it was the curious colours or the subject matter, but he had never seen anything like them.

Dr Dewbury returned with two bottles of Heineken. He handed one to Smith. "Are you into art?"

Smith took the beer. "No, but these are quite different." He pointed to one of the paintings. "This is in The Northern Territory isn't it?"

"I thought I detected a hint of an Aussie accent there. It is indeed. Does it make you think of home?"

"I grew up out west, so the bush isn't like that, but you've captured it perfectly."

"I can't take all the credit," Dr Dewbury said and took a long swig of beer. "The paint I use is very costly. Now, I don't think you're here to talk about art, are you? Is this about Kirsty? Have there been some new developments?"

"You could say that. Dr Dewbury, do you know a student called Taylor Fox? She's studying business studies."

"Please call me Henry – it is after hours after all, and yes, I do know Taylor. Why do you ask?"

Smith took a sip of beer and winced. He wasn't much of a lager fan.

"We believe she was due to attend a meeting with one of your faculty on Wednesday. Do you perhaps know who she was supposed to be meeting?"

"I'd scheduled a meeting for five," Dr Dewbury replied. "But Taylor didn't show up."

"So, she was due to meet you?"

"That's right."

Smith stood up. "Please excuse me, but I need to make a phone call." He left the room, walked down the hallway and stopped in the kitchen. He took out his phone, dialled the switchboard at the station, and informed the officer on duty that she was to contact the rest of his team and tell them to call off the visits to the other people in the law faculty.

"Sorry about that," Smith said and sat back down opposite Dr Dewbury. "You said that Miss Fox didn't turn up for the meeting?"

"That's right. I recall being rather annoyed about it at the time."

"Why is that?"

"Taylor had expressed a keen interest in business law, and I was only too happy to help her, but I suppose you can only help people so much. What is this all about?"

"I'm afraid Miss Fox is dead," Smith said. "She was found yesterday evening in an alleyway outside a pub. We believe she died sometime on Wednesday evening."

"Dead? How?"

"We're still looking into it. So, Miss Fox was due to meet you at five, and you say she didn't turn up?"

"That's correct. I waited until half past and went home. I do have better things to do than wait for time-wasters."

Dr Dewbury finished the beer in the bottle and rubbed his eyes. "God. Now I know why she didn't turn up. This is awful. First Kirsty and then Taylor. Do you believe their deaths are connected?"

"Like I said, we're looking into it."

"I need another beer," Dr Dewbury stood up and left the room.

Smith had only finished half of his Heineken but was handed another when Dr Dewbury returned.

"I can't believe this has happened," the Doctor of Law said. "In York of all places."

"How long have you been painting?" Smith decided to change the subject.

"Quite a while. It's my way of switching off at the end of the day. Mrs Dewbury used to hate my paintings – it's only since she departed, I've been allowed to actually hang them up."

"Your wife's dead?" Smith said. "I'm sorry."

"Don't be," Dr Dewbury laughed. "It would have been a hell of a lot cheaper if she'd snuffed it, believe you me. No, she decided to move on with an accountant. It's quite embarrassing really – not only does a Doctor of Law lose almost everything in a divorce settlement, he's replaced by a bloody accountant. Anyway, that's the reason for this humble abode. But it's home, and I can paint to my heart's content."

Smith finished what was left in the first bottle of beer and left the other one untouched on the table next to his chair.

"I won't disturb you any further," he said and stood up. "Thanks for the beer."

"I'm sorry I couldn't be much help," Dr Dewbury said. "Do you have any leads in the investigation?"

"We're following a number of lines of enquiry," Smith gave him the usual vague reply.

"That old chestnut. That usually means you've got sweet FA. Sorry, it's the bad, old lawyer coming out in me. I wasn't always a University man you know. Can I give you some advice?"

"Of course."

"I realise that as a detective you've come to distrust everybody you speak to, but you will get a lot further in your enquiries if you're a bit more open with the people you put your questions to. I get the feeling there's more to the deaths of these two young women than you're letting on, and by holding back this information you could be hindering the progress of the investigation. Take it with a pinch of salt if you like."

"I'll give it some thought," Smith said. "Thank you for your time."

CHAPTER NINETEEN

Smith opened the door to his house and went inside. The dogs were on him in a flash. Theakston, the rather overweight Bull Terrier was finding it hard to jump any further than his waist, but Fred, the repulsive Pug managed a leap halfway up Smith's chest.

"That's enough, you two," Smith said with a big grin on his face. "Where's my wife and child?"

"Heating up some stew in the oven," Whitton appeared in the doorway of the kitchen. "And that daughter of ours is sleeping off all the food she's just tucked away. That child is worse than Theakston. Beer?"

"Just what the doctor ordered. I'm going outside for a smoke."

"Did you find out anything from our Doctor of Law?" Whitton asked when Smith came back inside.

"Not much. He said that Taylor Fox asked him for a meeting to discuss business law, but she didn't show up."

"Do you believe him?"

"He seemed genuine, and he was definitely shocked when he found out about her murder. He gave me a piece of advice too."

"I bet that went down well."

"He reckons I hold back too much information when I question people, and he also thinks that if I offer a bit more, we'll get to the truth a hell of a lot quicker. I think that's what he meant – he was rather vague."

"I can't remember a time when you've ever taken a piece of advice," Whitton said."

"Maybe he has a point. Maybe if we make the blood thing public knowledge, it might jog someone's memory about something they didn't think was important before."

"What are you suggesting?" Whitton looked shocked. "A press conference? We are asking for information about somebody who likes to kill young women and drain their blood. Do you realise what kind of whackos that will bring out of the woodwork?"

"I don't know what I'm suggesting, Erica. I just know that what we have so far is a big fat zilch. We haven't found anything to link the two women together – we haven't found any evidence at either scene that we can use, and we don't even have a direction to head in at the moment. We've got nothing apart from two bloodless corpses and it's driving me nuts."

"Just calm down," Whitton said. "Every murder investigation you've ever brought to a conclusion had moments like this. Just remember that. You ought to know more than most that there is a stage in every case where all we have on our side is the urge to move past the desperation. That's what's kept you driven all these years. And, even though you might not think so, this investigation will be no different."

"If you say so."

"Do you remember what you said to the old lady? Taylor Fox's landlady?"

"What did I say?" Smith asked.

"She asked you if you were going to catch this killer and you told her you were without even thinking about it."

The alarm on the oven told them the stew was ready.

"Now," Whitton said. "Let's eat, and I won't hear any more of this negativity bullshit from you. It doesn't suit you."

"What was up with Bridge today?" Smith asked with a mouthful of stew. "His whole attitude stank."

"He'd arranged to have a few drinks with PC Baldwin, and he was worried he might have to miss out."

"Well, he's a DS now, so his womanising is going to have to take a back seat. This stew is delicious. I didn't know you could cook like this."

"My mum made it," Whitton admitted. "I just heated it up."

"Baldwin should know better than to risk anything with Bridge," Smith carried on. "She ought to know of his reputation by now."

"She's a big girl. I'm sure she can look after herself. Besides, Bridge isn't a bad looking bloke."

"He's funny-looking if you ask me, and don't forget his first name is Rupert. That's enough to put anyone off."

"You're terrible," Whitton said. "I forgot to tell you; I've arranged everything with Marge at the Hog's Head. She was more than happy to have your birthday there. She asked if we could make it an early evening thing. Around six."

"Sounds great."

"Thirty-six," Whitton said with a smile on her face. "That's knocking on for forty."

"No it's not, besides, you're not that far behind me."

"I haven't had chance to get you a present yet."

"I don't want one. Help me crack this investigation and that'll be more than enough. This really is an annoying one. Two women are dead, and we don't even have any suspects. That must be a first."

"I thought we weren't going to mention the case again tonight," Whitton said sternly.

"OK," Smith said. "I'll make you a deal. I'll get us a couple of beers – we go over it once more and I promise you won't hear another word from me about it until tomorrow morning. It'll be like old times."

"Very romantic. I get the feeling I don't have much choice in the matter, do I?"

"No. I'm just going out for a quick cigarette, and we can make a start."

"It's bloody freezing out there," Smith said when he came back inside. "Right, what are we missing here? Kirsty King was killed sometlme last weekend. We've ascertained that she almost certainly knew her killer. Conveniently, she was alone in her house the whole weekend. Taylor Fox died on Wednesday and she was dumped outside the pub on Friday. What does that tell us?"

"That whoever killed her must have held onto her for a couple of days after she was already dead," Whitton said.

"Right. Why did our killer do that? Why not just get rid of the body as soon as he'd killed her and drained her blood?"

"Maybe he didn't find the right opportunity," Whitton suggested."

"Possibly," Smith mused. "Taylor rented a room with the old lady – there was no evidence to suggest she was killed there, so we're faced with another problem."

"We're missing a crime scene."

"Exactly. The path guys are still busy with her, and we'll know more when they're finished, but I don't expect them to give us much. So, where do we go from here?"

"Motive," Whitton said.

"Always motive," Smith agreed. "And I'm beginning to formulate a theory about that."

"Go on."

"The way these women were killed wasn't particularly violent which would suggest the killing itself was just a means to an end."

"The blood?" Whitton said.

"The blood. That's what we'll concentrate on. Why would somebody possibly need so much blood? Don't hold back."

"Maybe it's a cult thing," Whitton suggested. "I've read about some of those weird cults, smearing themselves with blood and dancing naked in the moonlight."

Smith remained silent.

"You said don't hold back," Whitton said.

"No," Smith said. "I'm just thinking about what you said. We'll look into it. What else?"

"Vampirists. There are actually nutcases who like to drink human blood."

"I've heard about them. There are some real sickos out there. It looks like we've got some really interesting research on the agenda tomorrow."

"Can we stop with this topic of conversation now?" Whitton said. "I'm definitely going to have nightmares tonight."

"We need to seek the advice of a nutcase to help us catch a nutcase," Smith said out of the blue.

"You're talking about Jessica Blakemore again aren't you?" Whitton frowned. "You heard what the DI said about that idea."

"Brownhill won't even know about it – I just want to ask Jessica's opinion about a few things. She has proven to be very useful in the past."

"You're playing with fire. Crap, have you seen the time? It's past midnight. I think it's time for bed, and I'm definitely going to have nightmares tonight."

CHAPTER TWENTY

John Powell was almost knocked flying by an icy gust. The cold front that had gripped Scotland and parts of the north of England wasn't quite finished wreaking havoc yet. Snow was forecast for the higher ground later in the week, and people had been advised to stay indoors whenever possible.

John Powell was already in a foul mood, and the weather really wasn't helping. The pub and restaurant where he worked as landlord was expecting a busy day – a party of forty had booked for a champagne breakfast, and John's bar manager hadn't turned up for work. She wasn't answering her phone, so John, in a fit of fury had decided to take it upon himself to pay her a visit at home.

He pressed the buzzer next to the door and waited. The door was opened by a young man in a tracksuit who had clearly overdone it the night before. His eyes were mere slits in his head and his skin was pale and bluish around the eyes.

"Can I help you?" he said.

John recoiled from the stale alcohol on his breath. "I'm here to see Rene. Rene Downs. She works at my pub."

The man yawned and more beer fumes came out of his mouth. "I haven't seen her since Friday morning."

"Do you mind if I go up?" John pointed to the staircase.

"Be my guest. I'm off out for a run. See if I can sweat out some of the booze I drank last night."

John climbed the stairs and stopped outside Rene Downs' flat. He was about to knock on the door when he realised it was slightly ajar. He pushed it open slowly and glanced inside.

"Rene," he said. "It's John. You were supposed to be at work half an hour ago. Rene, Are you in there?"

No answer.

"Rene," John opened the door wider. "I really need you at the Green Man. We've got that big booking this morning, remember. Rene."

He went inside the room. Rene Downs was nowhere to be seen. The flat consisted of one medium-sized room that acted as living room and kitchen. A door on the left led to the only bedroom in the flat, and another door further along opened into a small bathroom.

"Rene," John said once more and took out his mobile phone. He dialled Rene's number and a few seconds later he heard the buzzing sound of a phone on vibrate-only coming from the kitchen-side of the room. The phone was attached to a plug in the wall and it was hopping along the worktop as it vibrated. John walked towards the door of the bedroom and pushed it open. The curtains were closed, but a sliver of sunshine peering through them cast a flickering light on the bed where Rene Downs was lying. She was on her back on top of the covers, and when John Powell saw her face, he felt a burning sensation in his stomach and staggered back a few feet. He backed out of the room, left the flat and ran down the stairs as though he was being chased by the ghost of the dead woman on the bed.

Smith and Yang Chu arrived fifteen minutes later. Grant Webber had slept late, but the Head of Forensics had promised to get there as soon as he could. John Powell was sitting with his face in his hands at the bottom of the stairs when Smith came in. He looked up when he realised Smith was standing there.

"Are you from the police?"

"DS Smith," Smith told him. "And this is DC Yang Chu. Are you the one who called it in?"

"John Powell. I'm the landlord of the Green Man on Pike Street. Rene runs the bar for me. When she didn't show up for work this morning I came to see if she was alright."

"Where is she?" Smith came straight to the point.

"In the bedroom in her flat. It's the last one along the corridor on the second floor. It was awful. Her face..."

"OK, Mr Powell, we're just waiting for a forensics team to arrive. Did you touch anything inside the flat?"

"Of course not. Why would I?"

"We'll need your fingerprints anyway. And we'll need a statement from you. When did you last see Miss Downs?"

"Friday night," John told him. "Just after closing time. I offered to call a taxi for her – I even offered to escort her home, but she insisted on walking. You don't think..."

"We don't think anything at the moment, Mr Powell. Do you know Miss Downs well?"

"She's been working at the Green Man for just over a year. She's a very hard worker."

"Is she full time there?"

"Just weekends. She's a student at the University."

Another one, Smith thought. *Another dead student.*

Grant Webber announced his presence with a cough. He was alone.

"What have we got?" he addressed the question to Smith.

"We don't know yet," Smith said and turned back to John Powell.

"We'll need to speak to you again, but you can get back to work now. I'll arrange for someone to get that statement."

"I can't get that picture out of my head," John said. "Her face. There was no life left in it."

"Let's have a look, shall we?" Smith said to Webber and they walked up the stairs.

"The bloke who found her said he didn't touch anything," Smith told the head of forensics outside Rene Downs' flat.

"That'll be a first," Webber handed Smith a SOC suit and a pair of gloves.

Smith took the suit but refused the gloves. "I'll use my own thank you. Your regular issue ones make my hands itch like crazy for hours afterwards."

They suited up and went inside the flat. Smith stopped in the middle of the living room–cum kitchen and looked around. The room was sparsely furnished but homely. A three-seater sofa was propped up against one of the walls. It looked old, but a woollen throw had been placed on it to cover the worn patches in the upholstery. A small TV stood on a large cardboard box opposite it. The kitchen side of the room was tiny, with only enough room for a two-plate stove, a small fridge and a microwave oven.

"Another student?" Webber said.

"How did you guess?" Smith said.

The smell inside Rene Down's bedroom hit Smith as soon as he and Webber went inside. It was unmistakable. And it was a smell he hoped he wouldn't have to experience again so soon – a tangy, metallic odour that entered the nostrils and seemed to linger there.

"Blood," Webber said. "Can you smell it?"

Smith didn't answer the question. He looked at the young woman on the bed. "I think we've got another one. Look at her face."

Rene Downs was staring up at the ceiling. Her eyes were fixed on the light fitting. Her mouth had a bluish tinge round the edges and her cheeks were white.

"How long do you reckon she's been lying here?" Webber asked.

"Rough guess."

"Around thirty hours," Smith said without hesitation.

"You sound pretty sure."

"It's hard to tell if her blood has been removed," Smith said. "But the man who found her told me she finished her shift after closing time on Friday and refused a taxi home. I'd say she was either followed home, or someone was waiting for her when she got back to her flat. That would put it at around half-past-midnight. We'll be able to pinpoint it when the path guys have finished, but I've got a feeling I'm right on this one. That plus the fact she's still wearing her uniform from the Green Man would suggest she was killed as soon as she got back here."

"I'm inclined to agree," the head of forensics said.

"Will you please stop agreeing with me, Webber. People are going to start thinking we like each other."

"Don't push it. It doesn't look like much of a struggle took place in here. Everything seems to be in its place."

Smith started to pace up and down the room. He stopped at the curtains, looked up at the light fitting in the ceiling and turned around to face Webber.

"He closed the curtains and turned off the light."

"What are you going on about?" Webber said.

Smith ignored him and walked back to the living room. The lights were off in there too.

"He turned out the lights in here too," he said to a bewildered looking Grant Webber. "If she was killed here in the early hours of Saturday morning the lights would have had to have been on. The man who found Rene didn't touch anything, so whoever killed her must have turned out the lights before he left. I'll leave you in peace to ponder over that thought. I need a smoke – that stench is starting to settle in my nostrils, and I need to get rid of it."

CHAPTER TWENTY ONE

It was not yet ten in the morning as Smith drove away from Rene Downs' flat and headed in the direction of the station. The streets were deserted – the nasty weather had obviously put people off venturing outside. Smith drove on autopilot. He'd driven these roads for years and he could navigate them blindfold. As he drove his thoughts drifted to the events of the past week.

Three young women had been killed.

All three of them had had their blood removed.

All three were students at the University.

A pattern was beginning to form in Smith's head and his heartbeat quickened slightly. His mind began to process the details of all three murders at lightning speed, and then it hit him.

"They all knew the murderer," he said to his reflection in the rear-view mirror. "All three of them. They knew him well and they didn't feel at all threatened in his presence."

He pulled over in a lay-by and turned off the engine.

They were all students, he thought. *They all attended the same University.*

They were killed by someone at that University.

Smith took out his phone and scrolled down his contacts. It had been a while since he had last called the person his finger stopped on. He pressed *call* and waited. He heard the sound of the dial tone on the other end for more than ten times and was about to end the call when a woman's voice was heard. She sounded either very wary or very bored.

"Hello."

"Jessica," Smith said. "It's Smith. I need to talk to you. Can we meet up?"

"Jason," Jessica said. "Firstly, I knew exactly who was calling – there is this thing called caller ID, and I very nearly didn't answer at all. What do you want?"

"You said, *firstly*," Smith said.

"What?"

"You said, *firstly*," Smith said once more. "Which usually indicates there is something to follow. In my experience, it's normally a, *secondly*. Well?"

"Secondly," Jessica humoured him, and Smith was sure he could sense a smile on her face one the other end of the line. "I thought I made it quite clear the other evening that my serial-killer-profiling days are over. I'm a lecturer at the University now and it suits me just fine. Find someone else to do your dirty work for you."

"But you're irreplaceable, Jessica. There is nobody quite like you."

"That kind of flattery probably gets you everywhere," Jessica said. "But not today. Not with me. Not ever. Goodbye, Jason."

"Wait," Smith said. "Please just listen to what I have to say. If you still feel the same when I've finished, I won't bother you ever again."

The line went quiet for a few seconds.

"Are you still there?" Smith asked.

"I'm still here," Jessica replied. "I was just musing over the promise you just made me. You won't bother me ever again you say?"

"Yes."

"Can I have that in writing?"

"Where are you now? This won't take long. I'll buy you breakfast."

* * *

The front of the Cafe no 8 Bistro on Gillygate had undergone a facelift since Smith was last there. It was now also named no8 Bistro. Smith went inside and looked around. Jessica Blakemore was sitting at the table closest to the window. A full cup of coffee sat on the table in front of her. Smith sat down opposite her.

"Thank you for agreeing to meet me."

"I know you, Jason," she said. "You wear people down until you get what you want. What's so urgent that only an ex-whack-job shrink can help you?"

"Let's eat breakfast first," Smith suggested. "What I'm about to tell you is not really something to discuss over a meal."

A waitress appeared with a couple of menus and Smith chose a full English breakfast and some strong coffee. Jessica opted for the vegetarian option.

"How are you keeping?" Smith asked when the waitress had gone.

"I'm putting the pieces of my life back together," Jessica replied. "And I was doing a great job of it until you threw a spanner in the works. I'm getting better one day at a time – I love the job at the University, and I'd quite like to keep that momentum going. I will not risk sinking back to where I was. Not for you, not for anybody."

"That's a bit melodramatic isn't it?"

"No, it isn't. My mind is still fragile, and after spending years safely tucked away from society, it's going to take a long time before I'm strong again. What about you?"

"I'm a family man now," Smith said proudly. "Family man through and through. There was even a time not so long ago I contemplated giving up the job altogether."

"You know that's never going to happen, don't you?"

"My priorities have changed, Jessica. As have my loyalties. I have a wife and beautiful daughter who need me, and that's a totally alien concept to me. The fact that there are people in the world who actually need me to come home from work safely every day has made me look at everything in a completely different light."

Jessica didn't say anything. She studied Smith's face intently for a while, and finally her facial muscles softened, and she smiled.

"You really have changed, haven't you?"

"I suppose it happens to all of us some day," Smith said. "I must be honest – I never expected it to happen to me."

The breakfasts arrived and they ate in silence. Snow was now falling softly against the window. The Chinese Takeaway on the opposite side of the road was closed, and there were very few people walking past. Smith placed his knife and fork on the plate and took a drink of coffee. Jessica had eaten everything on her plate.

"Your appetite has definitely improved since I last saw you," Smith commented. "How long have you been vegetarian?"

"I'm not," she replied. "I didn't feel like bacon and sausages. Now, spit it out."

"Excuse me?"

"What is it you want to talk to me about?"

"Three women have been killed in the past week," Smith said. "Three students from the University."

"I heard there were two," Jessica appeared shocked.

"I came straight here from the third one. Not a pretty sight."

"And how do you think I can help you?"

"I believe we're dealing with a rather depraved killer here."

"Surely anyone who murders another human being displays a certain depravity," Jessica said.

"I've seen a lot," Smith said. "I've seen the worst depravity the human mind is capable of, but I haven't seen anything like this before. These women were murdered. The killings weren't particularly violent or brutal, but it's what happened to the victims later that I'm still trying to come to grips with. All three of them had their blood drained from their bodies. Almost every last drop."

"I see," Jessica said.

It wasn't the reaction Smith was expecting.

"How was the blood drained?" Jessica asked.

"We found needle marks on two of them. It looks like whoever did this carried out a drastic blood transfusion. They were drugged first."

"Were all these women killed at home?"

"No," Smith said. "Well, the first one was, but the second one had been dead for a while when she was found outside a pub in town. We checked the house where she lived, and we found nothing to suggest she was killed there."

"And the third? You said there were three."

"It's too early to tell – like I said, I only left the scene a short while ago, but my gut is telling me she was killed inside her flat."

"They knew their killer," Jessica said.

"That's what I think."

"Then what do you need me for?"

"Hold that thought," Smith stood up. "I need a pee."

"Where were we?" Smith said when he sat down. "Oh yes. What do I need you for? I need you to help me to get inside the head of somebody who kills three young women and then takes their blood away with him. What do you make of that?"

"You're doing it again, Jason," Jessica said. "You assume you can give me a few snippets of information about a case and I'm going to pull the name of the killer out of a hat. It doesn't work like that. I need more."

"What do you need to know?"

"Did these women know each other?"

"No. They attended the same University, but they were all on different courses."

"You say there was no blood left inside them when they were found?"

"Every last drop was drained."

"That indicates a well-researched murderer. And meticulous planning. Do you realise how long it takes to remove the blood from an average person? And to perform a transfusion, that person has to be alive for most of the time."

"A good few hours," Smith said. "That's another reason we believe the victims knew the killer. I believe he gained access without arousing suspicion, and then he killed these women."

"You said he," Jessica said. "You always tend to assume that killers are men."

"He, she," Smith said. "It doesn't matter. I need you to think about why anyone would take someone's blood. What on earth would they gain from it?"

"I'll give it some thought," Jessica said. "Don't contact me. I'll phone you if I come up with anything."

"Thank you for your time," Smith said. "Breakfast is on me."

Jessica shook her head. "I'll just email the invoice for this consultation to your DI, shall I?"

"We don't need to involve Brownhill in this. I'll speak to you soon."

CHAPTER TWENTY TWO

Smith found Whitton, Bridge and Yang Chu in the canteen when he arrived at the station. Bridge and Whitton were looking at something on a laptop.

"Where have you been?" Yang Chu asked Smith. "Brownhill is going ballistic."

"I had an appointment I needed to keep." He walked behind Whitton and placed his hands on her shoulders. "What are you looking at?"

"Vampirism," Bridge replied. "And would you mind not pawing the DCs when you're at work."

"Are you still pissed off because you missed your hot date with Baldwin?"

"Pissed off doesn't even begin to describe it," Bridge said. "Baldwin's had time to think things over and she's decided it's not such a good idea after all."

"Never mind, Rupert," Smith patted him on the arm. "There's plenty more suckers in the sea. What the hell is that?"

On the screen on the laptop was a photograph of a young couple. They were no more than twenty years old – both were dressed entirely in black, but it was what they held in their hands that made Smith look twice at the screen.

"These oddballs really believe they can gain superiority through the drinking of blood," Whitton told him. "I didn't realise this kind of thing was so widespread. There are whole sub-cultures springing up with paying members. It's really quite sick."

"Are there any of these in York?" Smith asked.

"It's possible," Bridge said. "Any town with a big student population could breed one of these sub-cultures. In the eighties and nineties, it was Goths – these sickos just take the alternative lifestyle a couple of steps further. Students are easy pickings."

DI Brownhill came in and marched up to their table. "Get back to work, all of you. We're in the middle of a triple murder investigation and you're all lounging about in here."

"We are working, Ma'am," Yang Chu said. "We're looking into Vampirism on the Internet. It's much warmer in here than it is down in the offices."

"Smith," Brownhill said. "My office now."

She bounded out without saying another word.

"What have you done now?" Whitton asked.

"For once, I really can't think of anything," Smith replied. "Maybe it's something to do with my birthday tomorrow."

The expression on Brownhill's face told Smith straight away that Smith's birthday celebrations were the last thing on the DI's mind.

"Close the door and sit down," she bellowed.

Smith did as he was asked. "What's wrong, boss?"

"I've just had a most interesting interaction," Brownhill began. "From a future detective as it happens. A young man from one of the restaurants in town was very proud of the fact that he managed to do some amateur sleuthing and track you down to this station."

"I'm afraid I have no idea what you're talking about, boss."

Brownhill reached under her desk and held up a small handbag. "Do you recognise this?"

"I haven't carried one of those since my days in uniform."

"Don't be pedantic, Smith. It was left on the table you were sitting at not so long ago this morning. You had breakfast there - the young man who put your credit card transaction through recognised you from the newspapers and delivered the bag here personally. I happened to be speaking to someone at the front desk at the time. I assumed he'd made a mistake, so I checked the contents of the bag. What were you doing having breakfast with Jessica Blakemore when you were supposed to be on duty?"

"It seemed like a good idea at the time, boss," Smith said. "I thought she might be useful, but it turns out you were right. Nothing came of it. I should have listened to you, and I assure you it won't happen again. I'll get back to work then."

He smiled and stood up.

"Sit down. I'm not finished. What exactly did you discuss with Jessica?"

"I asked for her input into the whole blood thing," Smith said. "I asked her what she thought could make someone kill someone and take their blood. Like I said, she wasn't very helpful. And I won't be seeing her again."

"Make sure you don't. What have we got from this latest murder?"

"Rene Downs. She was another student at the University. She was last seen at around midnight on Friday. It was her boss at the pub she works in who found her this morning. He told us she left the bar after refusing a taxi home and walked to her flat. It's about a five-minute walk. My initial thoughts are she was either followed or someone was waiting for her when she arrived home."

"So, she was definitely killed at home?" Brownhill asked.

"Looks like it."

"Did Grant find anything at the scene?"

"He's still busy with it, but when we checked the place this morning the lights were off. If she was killed when she got home from work the killer would have needed the lights on, so I'm certain he switched off the lights when he was finished. Webber was about to check the switches for prints when I left."

"When you left to have breakfast with Jessica Blakemore?" the DI reminded him.

Smith couldn't think of a reply to that and he was relieved when his phone started to ring in his pocket. He took it out and looked at the screen. It was Dr Kenny Bean.

"Kenny," he answered it. "What's new?"

"We've done an initial on the young woman found dead this morning," the pathologist got straight to the point. "She was drained of blood, no doubt about that, and she's been dead a good twenty-four hours."

"Did you find any drugs in her system?" Smith asked. "Particularly Flunitrazepam or Benzodiazepine?"

"Hold your horses, Smith. We're good, but we're not that good. Tox reports take time, but if I were to hazard a guess, I'd say she was definitely injected with something. There was a needle mark on the back of her right leg."

"Thanks, Kenny," Smith said. "I owe you a drink."

"I like Single Malt," Dr Bean informed him. "And I doubt a detective sergeant's salary could stretch to that. I'll let you know as soon as we know more."

He rang off before Smith could say anything else.

"Progress?" Brownhill asked.

"Nothing that really gets us any closer, boss. That was Kenny Bean. He found what looks like a needle mark on Rene Downs' leg, and he thinks she could have been injected with something before her blood was taken."

"Three dead students," Brownhill sighed. "All of them with bright futures, and their whole lives ahead of them and now they're all lying in the morgue, bereft of blood. What the hell is going on in this town?"

"We'll catch this bastard, boss. I'm going to catch this bastard if it kills me."

CHAPTER TWENTY THREE

"What did the DI want?" Whitton asked Smith when he sat back down in the canteen.

"Some bastard wannabe detective informed her I had breakfast with Jessica Blakemore this morning," Smith told her.

"You did what?"

"We're running out of options, Whitton," Smith said, much louder than he intended. "And we're getting desperate. Whether you like it or not, Jessica is a highly qualified and astute psychiatrist."

"It's not about liking *it*," Whitton's voice had also increased in volume. "I just don't like *her*. You turn into a different person when you've been to see that woman."

"I do not. Do I have to remind you how many times she's helped me out in the past?"

"You never stop reminding me," Whitton stood up so abruptly that her chair was flung out behind her. "I'll be in my office if you need me. It may be colder down there, but the atmosphere in here is getting chillier by the minute."

Bridge and Yang Chu kept quiet. They were making a bad job of pretending to look at something on Bridge's laptop.

"That time of the month," Bridge finally broke the silence. "If you ask me, women shouldn't be allowed to occupy positions of power."

"That's probably the most male-chauvinistic bollocks that's ever come out of your mouth," Yang Chu said. "And that's quite an achievement where you're concerned."

"It's true," Bridge hadn't quite finished yet. "Or at least if they have to hold high-up positions, they should be forced to take a mandatory week off each month. It's not their fault – hormones can be a bastard."

Yang Chu was about to argue further when DCI Chalmers came in. He glanced in their direction, got some coffee from the high-tech machine in the corner and sat down next to Smith. He took a large sip of coffee, winced, removed the lid from a silver hip-flask and replaced what he'd drunk with an amber-coloured liquid.

"Rough morning, boss?" Smith asked.

Chalmers raised the hipflask to his lips, took a large sip and screwed the lid back on. "I didn't even want this bloody job. I only accepted the DCI post because Mrs Chalmers would have had my balls if she ever found out I'd turned it down. I'm no pen-pusher – I'm an old fashioned hard-arse detective, and between you and me, I'd take a demotion tomorrow if I could. Today is Sunday in case any of you are unaware. And as a DCI I should be lounging around at home, reading the Sunday papers or taking Mrs Chalmers out for a nice lunch, but I'm stuck in here drinking Scotch from a bloody hipflask."

"Nice speech, boss," Smith said. "This has something to do with old Smyth doesn't it?"

"You're bloody right it does. That public-school amoeba will drive me to a nuthouse one day. He came back early, and with his crime stats presentation coming up, he wanted to go over everything two days prior to make sure we don't look foolish in front of the press."

"I thought you said it was Smyth who invited the press in the first place."

"It was," Chalmers finished half of his coffee in one go. "And that old imbecile couldn't come across as anything but foolish if he tried, but he wants to go all out this year." He handed Smith the hipflask. "You might need a drop of this yourself when I tell you how your day is going to begin tomorrow. It's all in an email, but he wants you to head up a section about this ongoing triple murder investigation. He's scheduled a meeting between himself, you and Neil Walker tomorrow morning at ten. You know the Super doesn't show his face too early. He wants to reassure the public that we're doing everything in our power to bring this matter to its swift conclusion."

"Smyth's words?" Smith said and handed the hipflask back to the DCI.

"Smyth's words."

"But we've got nothing to go on right now," Smith said. "What am I supposed to tell the press?"

"That's the press liaison officer's department," Chalmers said. "Walker is very good. Knowing him, he'll just advise you to say as little as possible. You must have something. Three murders and you're telling me you've got nothing?"

"That's about the size of it. We don't have any suspects – no physical evidence, and no motive apart from the blood. And we're still no closer to figuring out what someone would want with so much blood."

"We're looking into weird cults and sub-cultures," Yang Chu said. "You wouldn't believe how many weirdoes there are out there. People who think by drinking human blood they will reach some kind of spiritual enlightenment."

Chalmers frowned at the young DC. "Could I have that once more in English please?"

"There are people out there who believe human blood holds some kind of power, and by drinking it they think this power will be transferred to them. It's all hocus-pocus, but it's pretty much all we've come up with so far."

"It's all beyond me," Chalmers drained what was left in his coffee cup. "I'm off home before the Super catches up with me. Keep plugging away. Something will turn up. I'll see you all tomorrow."

"I miss Chalmers," Bridge said. "He could be a real cantankerous git at times, but he was fair and what you saw was what you got. What's the plan of action?"

He addressed the question to Smith.

"Like Chalmers said," Smith said. "We keep plugging away. We look deeper into this sub-culture thing. This all has something to do with the University. The three dead women were students there, so that's where we look. Who would be the best person to talk to, to find out if York University has some secret cult operating there?"

"The Student Union rep?" Bridge suggested. "When I was at Uni the student rep knew everything that was going on around campus."

"We'll start there then," Smith agreed. "I think you can call it a day. I'm going to see if my wife is still friends with me, then I'm going to find out who the Student Union rep is and pay him a quick visit. Don't forget there's a thing at the Hog's Head for my birthday tomorrow."

CHAPTER TWENTY FOUR

The artist glanced at the sealed container next to the easel. The liquid inside filled the clear four-litre bucket almost to the brim.

"More than enough."

The latest blank canvas was small – small enough to spare the life of another young woman for the time being at least, but this was to be a special painting. A special painting for a special person. And afterwards the hunt would become much trickier and much more dangerous.

But this is how it has to be, the artist thought and carefully removed the lid from the bucket. *For real art to be worth anything, there is always a price to pay.*

The blown-up photograph was on the wall beyond the easel. The Pinnacles Desert, Western Australia. The photograph depicted a barren landscape of jagged limestone rock formations dotted around a sunburned wasteland. The sun was about to set and the shadows under the violent sandy formations were small.

The artist gazed at the photograph, hypnotised. Every indentation in the dead landscape was memorised. Every shadow and sharp edge was soaked up. The artist's eyes closed, and the image became even clearer.

Now, with eyes wide open the first exquisite brushstrokes caressed the canvas and the scene in the photograph slowly came to life. Then, the artist became bolder, and the strokes of the brush more violent until suddenly the artist had to stop the hand holding the brush with a swipe from the empty hand.

"Easy, easy," the artist said and took a number of deep breaths in quick succession. "It will all be alright in the end."

Art that is meant to be, the artist reflected, *will be.*

CHAPTER TWENTY FIVE

Smith found Whitton by the front desk. She was talking to Baldwin. From the expressions on both of their faces, Smith could see straight away that it was a pretty serious conversation. They stopped talking as soon as they spotted him.

"Sorry to interrupt," Smith said. "What's going on?"

"Girl stuff," Whitton said and smiled. "You know, clothes, makeup, that sort of thing."

"You're a terrible liar. Bridge has come up with an idea. He seems to think that whoever runs the Student Union might be able to shed some light on the seedier side of student life. I'm going to find out who it is and pay them a visit. Do you want to come with me?"

"Is that an order?"

"No," Smith replied. "But I'd quite like it if you came along."

"What were you and Baldwin really talking about back there?" Smith asked Whitton as they drove out of the car park at the station. Smith had called Henry Dewbury and found out the address for the Student Union representative. The head of the law faculty had been more than happy to help.

"That's none of your business," Whitton said. "I'm also allowed to have a few secrets you know."

"I don't keep secrets from you."

"What about your meeting with Jessica Blakemore?"

"I told you about that." Smith reminded her.

"Only because the DI busted you. If Brownhill hadn't found out, you wouldn't have told me would you?"

"It was a waste of time anyway. I think I'm beginning to see what you and Brownhill keeping going on about. Jessica isn't who she used to be

– she's a University lecturer and that's all. I suppose I was getting desperate. Are we okay?"

"Of course we're okay."

"Do you want to hear something funny?" Smith said, relieved.

"Knock yourself out."

Smith told her about Bridge's opinion on women in high-power positions.

Whitton started to laugh. "I can't believe he really thinks that. Seriously? Women should be forced to take a week off each month? No wonder Bridge is always single. That's something a Yorkshireman would have come up with fifty years ago."

As they approached the University campus, greyish-brown clouds had gathered overhead.

"It's going to snow," Whitton said. "I hope it settles – Laura hasn't seen much snow before, and I'd love to see what she does."

"If she's anything like the dogs she'll run away as soon as it starts to fall," Smith said. "This is the place here."

He parked on double yellow lines outside one of a row of houses that ran the whole length of the street.

"I hope this doesn't turn out to be another waste of time," Smith said as they got out of the car. "This whole investigation has been one waste of time after another."

"What did I say to you about this negativity crap," Whitton said sternly. "It really doesn't suit you."

Smith knocked on the door of the address Dr Dewbury had given them, and the door was opened by a woman who appeared to be in her early twenties. Smith couldn't be too sure. Her face was deathly pale – her ears were pierced more times than Smith could count, and her hair was dyed an unnatural black. Her eyes were heavily made up in black, one of her eyebrows had been shaved and steel studs had been inserted. She looked Smith and Whitton up and down and finally made eye contact with Smith.

"Good afternoon," he said. "Sorry to trouble you on a Sunday. I'm DS Smith and this is DC Whitton. We're looking for Bobby Hunt. Is he in?"

"What's this all about?" the woman asked, her eyes never leaving Smith's.

There was a crash from inside the house and the sound of laughter followed.

"We need to ask a few questions," Smith said. "Is Mr Hunt here?"

The woman's face softened, and she smiled. "No, there's no Mr Hunt here, but you can speak to me. Roberta Hunt. Bobby sounds much more student-like, don't you think? Henry warned me you were on your way. You'd better come inside; it looks like we're in for some snow."

Smith and Whitton followed her inside. People were dotted around the house. On the stairs, in the hallway, in the kitchen, the house was full of people. Most of them shared Bobby Hunt's idea of fashion, and black appeared to be the order of the day. Men and women alike wore similar black makeup to Bobby Hunt, and there wasn't a suntan in sight.

If we're looking for vampires, Smith thought. *We've come to the right place.*

"Sorry about the chaos," Bobby said. "We had a live band on at the Union last night and most of the band and half the audience ended up back here. We can talk in my room."

She opened up a door at the end of a corridor and gestured for Smith and Whitton to go inside.

Bobby Hunt's room was clean and smelled fresh. The bed was made, and there was no mess on the floor. A huge bookshelf covered one of the walls. When Smith had a closer look he noticed that the paperbacks on the shelf were all in alphabetical order. The majority of the books appeared to be crime thrillers and horrors. Two plastic chairs stood next to a large window.

Bobby closed the door. "Please take a seat. What's this about? Is there a problem at the student union?"

Smith sat on one of the two plastic chairs. Whitton pulled up the other one.

"This is going to sound a bit odd," Smith began. "But we actually need your help. As the student union rep, we thought you might be more clued up than most about what goes on after hours on campus."

Bobby started to laugh. "Sorry, but student union rep is so nineties. I'm actually the president of the student union. I was elected and I attend to the needs of the students. It's all democratic. What do you need to know?"

"Sorry for the misunderstanding. It's been a while since I was a student. We're investigating a string of murders involving students at this University."

"I am aware of them."

"What I'm about to say is very delicate. And I would appreciate it if this didn't go any further until we're absolutely sure of certain factors."

"I understand. Go on."

"We have reason to believe these murders were carried out by the same person, and we also have reason to believe they are all linked to the University in some way."

"I see," Bobby's brow creased and the studs in her eyebrow moved closer together. "*They are all*?"

"Excuse me?"

"You said you believe *they are all* linked to the University. Not *both of them*. Are you telling me there has been another one? I thought there had been two murders."

"I'm afraid another student was found dead this morning," Whitton told her.

"Oh my God. Who was it?"

"Her name will be released when her family have been informed," Smith said. "These murders all had one thing in common, and this is where your absolute discretion comes in. All three of these women had their blood drained from their bodies."

This information seemed to take a while for Bobby Hunt to digest. Her gaze shifted from Smith to Whitton and then back to Smith again.

"They had their blood drained?"

"That's right," Smith said. "And that brings us to the reason we're here. We know there are certain sub-cultures at large all around the country that advocate the drinking of human blood. They believe it offers them some kind of superior power. Are you aware of any such cults here in York? What are they called? Goths?"

"Drinking human blood?" Bobby's eyes widened. "Of course not. And I very much doubt that someone who drinks human blood would openly advertise the fact."

"I know it sounds far-fetched, Bobby," Whitton said. "But we had to ask. Do you know of anyone we could speak to who might be able to help us?"

"Why did you actually come here today?" Bobby's frown returned.

"Because I'm the president of the student union, or because of the way I dress? I won't always be dressed like this, and the piercings will have to be taken out, but right now I look like this because I can. And everybody you walked past in the hallway outside thinks the same way. Those *Goths,* as you called them are probably heading for first class degrees. Some of them are working towards MA's and the woman who was sitting at the bottom of the stairs with the tattoo of a snake where she's shaved off half of her hair is about to finish her PHD. We have a few years of this, and then we'll be thrown out into the real world to conform. You cannot begrudge..."

"You've got the wrong end of the stick there, Bobby," Smith cut her short. "You're not the first student to think like this and you certainly won't be the last. We had no idea what you looked like when we knocked on your door. We didn't even know if you were male or female, and to be honest, we couldn't give a monkey's arse. We're here because three young women have been killed, and we'd quite like to catch the bastard responsible before they do it again. Thank you for your time, Miss Hunt. If you do think of anyone who might be able to help us, give me a call."

He took out one of his cards and threw it on the desk next to a laptop computer. Bobby Hunt stood, speechless.

"We'll see ourselves out."

CHAPTER TWENTY SIX

"I think she touched a nerve back there," Whitton said as Smith drove away far too quickly from Bobby Hunt's house.

"Do these jumped up idealists think nobody has ever thought like them before, Whitton? Do they think they're the first? Do they really believe that just because we're police, we're a bunch of judgemental fascists? I really do bloody hate students."

"Calm down. And where are you going?"

"I'm killing two birds with one stone. Maybe three. I'm hungry – I really feel like a pint, and we're going to take your mum and dad out to lunch to say thanks for looking after Laura all the time."

"Well slow down then. I'd quite like to get there in one piece. And I'd better give my parents some warning. You know how my dad won't go out on a Sunday unless he's had a shower and there's a freshly-ironed shirt to wear. I'd quite like to go home and change too if that's alright."

It was snowing quite heavily when Smith and Whitton got out of the car at the Hog's Head pub. Whitton's parent's car was already parked. Smith and Whitton made their way through the blizzard inside the pub, and a wave of warm air hit them. Smith shook the snow from his coat and hung it on the coat rack by the entrance to dry. They made their way to where Whitton's parents were sitting. Laura was drawing something in a notebook on a blanket on the floor. Harold Whitton stood up when he spotted Smith and held out his hand.

"You don't have to get up on my account," Smith shook the hand. "I'm not used to people doing that."

"Common manners," Harold said and sat back down again. "Pint?"

"I'll get them. Good afternoon, Mrs Whitton. Thank you so much for having Laura. We really appreciate it. Can I get you a drink?"

"Just a half, love," Jane Whitton replied. "And please call me Jane. Mrs Whitton makes me feel old."

"And will you stop thanking us for spending time with that beautiful lady," Harold added and pointed to Laura.

She hadn't even looked up from her picture.

"What are you drawing there?" Smith knelt down besides his daughter. "Is that a cow?"

"Fred," Laura said perfectly clearly.

Smith looked again at the picture on the paper and realised it did bear a slight resemblance to the repugnant Pug. He kissed Laura on the top of her head and breathed in deeply. He wished he could bottle that scent.

"I'll order us some drinks," he said and approached the bar.

Marge was stock-taking behind the counter, and only spotted Smith at the last minute.

She looked up and grinned. "I see I've got the whole clan here this afternoon. It really is lovely to see. Pint?"

"Three and a half please, Marge."

"I'll have someone bring them over. What's the occasion? I thought your birthday wasn't 'til tomorrow."

"It's not – I just thought I'd treat Whitton's parents for all the times they've taken Laura off our hands."

Marge shook her head. "You'll see in time, love. They're not doing you a favour - it's actually the other way around. You'll understand when you're a grandparent yourself. I'll have someone bring the drinks over."

"You look tired, Jason," Jane said to Smith when he sat down. "You're working too hard."

"He's always working too hard," Whitton said. "He can't help himself. We're in the middle of a rough investigation."

"No leads?" Harold put the question to Smith, and it surprised him. Harold Whitton rarely showed any interest in their jobs.

"Very few," Smith admitted. "And nothing really to point us in any definite direction."

"Something will jump out at you, son. Just keep at it. I'm starving. I quite fancy that gammon special up on the board."

"My husband is having a steak and ale pie," Whitton joked.

"Don't be so presumptuous," Smith said. "I might surprise you one day."

"What are you having then?"

"The steak and ale pie," Smith said.

The Hog's Head was slowly filling up. Despite the nasty weather, people were venturing out for a good old-fashioned Sunday lunch. Smith spotted somebody he recognised at the bar. It was Dr Kenny Bean. He was talking to someone. It was clearly a woman but she had her back to Smith so he couldn't see her face. Dr Bean's face was strained and the way his hands moved around, Smith could see it wasn't a friendly conversation. The woman turned around and Smith realised who she was. It was Dr Dessai, the old Head of Pathology. Smith watched as they carried on talking – the conversation had obviously reached its crescendo, a drink was knocked over and Dr Dessai walked away from the bar. She marched past Smith's table, glared at him and stormed out of the pub.

"I wonder what that was all about," Jane Whitton had obviously noticed the disturbance at the bar too.

"I'm going to find out," Smith said and headed towards where Kenny Bean was busy clearing up pieces of broken glass.

"Be careful there," Smith warned. "You might cut yourself."

"I'll have one of the staff fetch a dustpan and brush," Marge added. "Accidents happen."

Dr Bean glanced up at Smith and frowned. He was clearly quite embarrassed about the whole scene – his face was red, and his hands were shaking.

"Are you alright?" Smith asked him.

"It was something over nothing. Dr Dessai and I merely had a difference of opinion."

"It looked like more than that to me. What's going on between you two?"

"I'd rather not discuss it," Dr Bean said. "If it's alright with you."

"No worries. I just wanted to see if you were alright."

"Thanks. I'll be better after a few pints."

"I'll leave you to it then," Smith could see that Dr Bean was in no mood for company.

"Friend of yours?" Harold asked Smith when he returned to the table.

"Kenny Bean," Smith told him. "He's Head of Pathology at the hospital."

"Best to stay out of it, love," Jane offered a piece of advice. "It doesn't do to get in the middle of relationship troubles."

The food arrived and the incident at the bar wasn't brought up again. When they were all finished Marge approached their table.

"Was everything alright?"

"Delicious," Harold said. "Absolutely delicious. Best gammon I've had in years."

"The steak and ale pie was perfect as usual, Marge," Smith added.

"We'd best be off," Harold announced and drained what was left in his glass. "There's a football game I want to watch on soon."
He took out his wallet.

"Put that away," Smith ordered. "I told you, this is our treat."

"Thanks, love," Jane added. "It was a lovely lunch."

"We'd better make a move too," Whitton said. "That little lady can hardly keep her eyes open."

She pointed to Laura on the blanket. She was sitting up – her eyelids were drooping and every now and again she would lunge forwards and wake up again.

"Do you mind going on without me?" Smith asked. "I need to talk to Kenny about something."

"Always working," Harold sighed. "It's admirable, but it'll wear you out sooner or later."

"I won't be long," Smith promised.

CHAPTER TWENTY SEVEN

Smith walked back inside the Hog's Head and headed straight for the bar. He'd been outside helping Whitton to secure Laura safely in the car.

Kenny Bean was still sitting at the bar.

"Can I get you a drink?" Smith offered.

The Head of Pathology looked at Smith and a smile appeared on his face. "I thought you'd left. A pint of Guinness would be great."

Smith could tell from the bloodshot eyes and the slurred diction that Dr Bean had already had quite a few.

"We had a bit of a thing at one stage," he said. "Rani and I."

"Rani?" Smith said.

"Dr Dessai. It was always going to be a bad idea. No offence, but relationships in the workplace seldom work out."

"No offence taken. I completely agree with you."

"It didn't last long," Dr Bean continued. "Around six months or so, and it ended amicably. Or so I thought."

"I see," Smith could sense there was more to it than that. "Go on."

"I don't know if I ought to tell you this. I don't even know why I told you what I have already."

Probably because of the five pints of Guinness you've just knocked back, Smith thought.

"What you tell me will go no further," he assured.

"Can we move to a table?" Dr Bean asked. "I'd feel more comfortable sitting at a table."

They sat at the table recently vacated by Smith and Whitton's family.

"Where do I start?" Dr Bean asked and Smith noticed that his left eye had moved closer to his right one.

"The beginning is always a good place," Smith suggested.

"Rani was head of department at the time," Dr Bean began. "She'd risen up the ranks quickly and she proved to be a very efficient leader. We worked long hours together, days and nights, and I really did enjoy working with her. One night we'd just finished a particularly gruelling fourteen-hour night shift – we were both dog-tired, but Rani suggested a coffee at her place. I accepted the offer, and things just seem to escalate from there. We were very happy together most of the time."

"What happened?" Smith asked. "What happened to cause this obvious atmosphere between you two?"

"I need to use the Gents. Guinness always does tend to go straight through me."

Smith was intrigued. Something about the way Dr Kenny Bean had opened up to him had piqued his interest. He had worked with Dr Dessai on a number of investigations, but he'd never shared the same confidence in her that he'd had with her predecessor, Paul 'The Ghoul' Johnson and now with the current head of Pathology, Dr Kenny Bean.

Kenny returned from the toilets visibly relieved.

He sat down again. "That's better. Where were we?"

"You were about to tell me what happened with Dr Dessai."

"Ah, yes. Rani. This is to go no further than this room today."

"I promise. You have my word."

"Because," Kenny looked Smith directly in the eyes. "Because if this does get out, I will not only become the laughing stock of the hospital, it could cost me my career."

"I told you," Smith said. "My lips are sealed."

Kenny took a long swig of Guinness and wiped the froth from his lips. "It started a few months or so into our relationship. Rani and I continued to work closely together despite our newly acquired personal situation. I began to notice that things were disappearing from the lab. Scalpels, and the like, and I didn't pay it much attention at first. Then other, more disturbing things started to go missing."

"Disturbing?" Smith pressed.

"Blood. I'd been working particularly long hours at the time, so initially I put it down to lack of sleep. You know how the mind works when you're worn out, but it carried on and I realised it wasn't my mind playing tricks on me – somebody was removing blood from the lab."

"Blood?" Smith couldn't believe what Dr Bean was telling him. "What would someone do with blood?"

"I'm getting to that. The volumes of blood we had in the lab were not large – maybe a few hundred millilitres at a time, but somebody was helping themselves to them, nevertheless. And one evening I found out who."

"Don't tell me," Smith said. "Dr Rani Dessai."

"Right. She was taking blood from the lab, and I caught her red-handed if you'll excuse the pun."

Smith looked at him and frowned.

"Blood? Red-handed? Never mind. Rani didn't even attempt to deny it. She couldn't – I'd watched her place three vials of blood in her bag. I was faced with the worst moral dilemma of my career. I knew I should report her. What I'd seen was indisputable, and I also knew that if it came out later that I kept it to myself, I would find myself in the dole queue in a flash."

"But you didn't report her, did you?"

"No," Kenny said with obvious regret. "I didn't. What would you have done in my place? Rani and I were a couple. We were getting on better than ever and we were even talking about maybe moving in together. I let my heart get in the way of rational thought."

"I'm not going to judge you for that, Kenny," Smith said. "I'd probably have done exactly the same thing if it had been me."

"Rani and I had a long discussion," Kenny continued. "It lasted all night, and we both agreed that she should request a transfer to another department. After what I'd seen, it was the only thing she could do. I promised her I would forget about what she'd done, and she promised it would never happen again. But of course, it didn't turn out to be that simple."

"It never is where women are concerned," Smith mused.

"No, Rani moved to another department, but what we had was doomed to fail. We started arguing all the time, and one day enough was enough and I ended the relationship. Rani has despised me ever since. So that's the story. Happy now?"

"Not really," Smith said. "You still haven't told me what she wanted the blood for."

"Oh, yes. The blood. You're going to find this very hard to believe, but Rani stole the blood to use as paint. She's always been an amateur artist, and she heard about a new trend in art where the materials used to paint were once alive. It's all very macabre if you ask me, but that's why she did it. Dr Rani Dessai risked everything she'd worked for because she wanted to experiment with a new form of art."

CHAPTER TWENTY EIGHT

"Paint?" Whitton looked at her husband as if he'd had much more to drink than he actually had.

Smith had arrived home and told her about what Dr Kenny Bean had said. Smith had made his excuses and left as soon as he could, leaving a very dejected-looking Doctor of Pathology in his wake.

"This is to go no further, though," he added. "The bit about doctor Dessai. I promised Kenny I wouldn't tell anyone."

"Are you seriously saying there are people out there who paint with human blood?" Whitton was obviously still finding this hard to digest.

"Apparently there are. This could be the break we've been looking for. So far we've had no idea about why someone would kill a person and remove their blood and now we have."

Whitton seemed to think hard for a moment. "Do you think Dr Dessai has anything to do with all this?"

"Of course not. She was caught stealing small quantities of blood from a lab. The blood taken from all the recent victims amounts to fifty-times what she took."

"Maybe she's upped her game a notch," Whitton said. "Maybe she needs more to paint bigger paintings."

"Don't be ridiculous, Erica. There's a big difference between pocketing a few vials of blood and killing someone and removing eight to ten pints. Besides, I told you I gave Kenny my word."

"Like he gave his word to a sicko who uses blood as paint. Have you heard yourself? We need to speak to this woman."

"I said no. Kenny could lose his job if this gets out."

"He shouldn't have let her get away with it in the first place."

"What would you expect me to do?" Smith said in a calm voice. "If we were faced with something similar? Would you expect me to ruin your life over some stupid mistake? They were in a relationship at the time."

"Don't you even try and compare that depraved woman with me," Smith's calm voice hadn't had the desired effect. "You know deep down that we need to bring her in and question her. This, *I gave him my word*, bollocks just doesn't wash. If I'd come home with the same story, you're telling me now, you'd pin the label, *suspect* on her in an instant."

Smith sighed. "You're right. You're right as usual, I would. It's just a really tricky one. How do I approach Dr Dessai without it coming out that I've betrayed Kenny's confidence?"

"OK," Whitton said. "Let's put it another way. How would you live with yourself if it turned out that Dr Dessai had something to do with these murders and you did nothing?"

"Fuck it. I need a strong drink."

"That's always the answer with you, isn't it? A strong drink."

"Excuse me?"

"That's your remedy for anything you can't face," Whitton said. "Whether it's work, personal or life in general. Chucking whiskey down your neck is always the cure."

Smith was about to say something further but realised that more than enough fuel had been added to the fire already. He went through to the kitchen, opened the cupboard and took out a full bottle of Jack Daniel's. He unscrewed the top and took a long swig straight out of the bottle. The warm, amber liquid warmed his throat as it went down and settled with a burn in his stomach. He opened the back door and with the bottle still in his hand he went into the back garden to smoke a cigarette.

The light upstairs in the main bedroom was switched on. Smith lit a cigarette and inhaled deeply. By the time he'd exhaled the first lungful of smoke, the light upstairs had gone out. Whitton had gone to bed. "Damn it," Smith spat the words out and took another mouthful of whiskey. "I've been so stupid."

He'd placed himself in an impossible position. His head was telling him that everything Whitton had said was the logical thing to do. They needed to bring Dr Dessai in for questioning even if it was for the sole purpose of eliminating her and moving on, but in doing so, he would be betraying the confidence of someone he had the greatest respect for. Kenny Bean would never trust him again. Yet if what Whitton pointed out happened, and it transpired that Dr Dessai was somehow involved in the recent murders and it came out that Smith was aware of her past transgressions, he wouldn't be able to live with himself. It was the worst of all catch-22 situations.

"There must be a way around it," he carried on talking out loud.

By the time Smith went back inside the whiskey in the neck of the bottle of Jack Daniel's was gone. Smith knew he should head upstairs to bed – tomorrow was going to be a long day, and he didn't want to feel hungover for his birthday, but he suddenly felt wide awake. He went to the living room and switched on his computer. If he was going to suffer the next day he wanted to at least have something to show for it. He put the bottle of whiskey on the desk next to the keyboard and waited for the old PC to boot up. The only sounds inside the house were the snorts and grunts coming from the two dogs on the sofa.

Smith opened up his search engine and typed in the words, *human blood and art* in the search bar. He was astounded by the results.

There were websites, Facebook pages and a whole list of artists who had been known to use human blood in their work. Smith scrolled down the list and shuddered. There were some photographs of artwork actually painted using blood. Some of them were quite disturbing. One of them in particular caught Smith's eye. It was a fairly small piece depicting a group of emaciated, bald heads. Eyes were bulging out of their sockets in some of the heads but most of them were almost skull-like. Smith was surprised that the colour of the blood on the canvas was more reddish-orange than the blood-red he'd expected. "This is just sick," he whispered. "What the hell goes on in the heads of the people who paint this stuff?"

He clicked on a link to the history of blood in art and began to read. The practice of using human blood went back millennia. There was evidence that some stone paintings depicting animals and early man, contained pigments of blood in the paint used. More recently, artwork created using human blood had sold for ridiculous prices to private buyers. The majority of galleries refused to display paintings containing human blood for health and safety reasons. By the time Smith had finished reading his stomach was warm and he was starting to feel slightly sick. He got up and went to the kitchen to make the strongest coffee he could handle. While he waited for the kettle to boil, he went outside to smoke the final cigarette of the day.

He took the coffee back to the living room and sat down in front of the computer screen again.

Blood and art, he thought as he read some more articles on the subject.

He sipped the coffee and grimaced. He'd made it far too strong. The alcohol in his system suddenly seemed to take effect. The writing on the screen was blurred, and even if he blinked, he couldn't make out whole sentences. His eyelids now felt incredibly heavy. He glanced at the painting of the malnourished half-heads painted in blood and then his thoughts drifted somewhere else.

CHAPTER TWENTY NINE

Smith woke up with a jolt when he felt a hand on his back. He opened his eyes and stared at the blank screen in front of him. The screensaver on the monitor had kicked in hours ago.

"Have you been here all night?" It was Whitton.

Smith rubbed his eyes. There was a half-empty coffee cup on the desk.

"I must have fallen asleep on the keyboard. It feels like there's a backwards QWERTY on my forehead."

"Happy Birthday," Whitton said. "I'll make some coffee. It looks like that one went cold hours ago."

Smith went upstairs to the bathroom and splashed some cold water on his face. He didn't dare look in the mirror to check if the keyboard had indeed left an imprint on his head. The nauseous feeling in his stomach and the pounding in his head already told him his face would look like death warmed up. He closed his eyes and muttered the words, 'Happy Birthday'.

He was now thirty-six-years old.

His body felt older. Much older.

"Sorry about being a bit of an arsehole last night," Smith said when he walked inside the kitchen.

Whitton had placed two large mugs of coffee on the table.

"I got a bit carried away with the loyalty crap. I couldn't bear to let Kenny down. I made a promise."

"And it's very honourable of you," Whitton said matter-of-factly.

"But I think I've come up with a way out," Smith added.

"Go on."

"The only people who know about Dr Dessai and the incident with the blood are Kenny Bean, you, me and Dr Dessai herself. You're right, we need to bring her in and interview her, but we do it under the pretence of expanding on what I'm going to bring up in the briefing this morning."

"I didn't understand a word of that," Whitton said.

"I'll put forward the possible motive for the murders," Smith carried on. "The use of blood as paint. And we'll bring in Dr Dessai, not only because of her expertise in the field of pathology, but because she's an amateur artist. Voila – two experts in one."

"Have you suddenly become wiser now you're a year older? That might just work though."

"And," Smith wasn't finished yet. "Nobody has to know about her previous infractions and she's hardly likely to want to bring it up herself, is she?"

"Not if she values her career," Whitton agreed. "There's just one problem. Won't that cause friction between her and Kenny Bean?"

"I don't think that's possible. I think the friction between them has passed the critical mass stage. Of course, I'll put it to Kenny first, but I can't see any reason why he'll disagree with me. He knows the score and he's probably expecting it, especially after what he told me last night."

The dogs ambled through and Theakston banged into the back door as a subtle hint that he needed to go outside. Smith opened it and the Bull Terrier ambled out into the back garden. Fred, the gruesome Pug trailed after him.

"Those dogs need more exercise," Whitton commented.

"When the weather warms up a bit. Theakston doesn't like the cold now he's in the autumn years of his life."

A dull thud on the doormat announced the arrival of the Monday morning post.

"I'll get it," Smith offered, and walked down the hallway.

He returned with a bundle of letters and a book-sized parcel wrapped in brown paper. He placed them all on the kitchen table.

"What's that?" Whitton pointed to the parcel.

Smith picked it up again. It had the words, *Jason Smith – Happy Birthday* written on the front and that was it. There was no address and no indication of where it had come from.

"What did you get me," Smith looked at Whitton and then at the parcel. "You told me you hadn't bought me anything."

"It's not from me," Whitton said. "Really, it isn't."

"There's no address on the front, so it must have been hand-posted before the other mail arrived. It wasn't there when I came down the stairs just now so it must have been posted very recently."

"Open it," Whitton said. "Don't just stand there pretending to be a detective – open it."

Smith tore at the tape on the back of the package, and carefully unwrapped it. The first thing he saw was the back of a small picture frame. He turned it around and gasped.

"What is it?" Whitton asked.

Smith showed her the painting. "If I'm not mistaken, this is the Pinnacles. It's a semi-desert a short trip inland from where I grew up. We used to go there sometimes in the school holidays. Why would someone send me this?"

"And more importantly, who?" Whitton said. "Usually when you send a birthday gift, you at least indicate who it's from. There's no name here, nothing."

Smith looked carefully at the painting. It definitely depicted the desolate landscape of the Pinnacles Desert. He hadn't set foot there in years, but he remembered the jagged limestone formations like it was yesterday.

"This is really weird," he said and put the painting down. "Why on earth would someone give me this for my birthday? And how would they even know I used to go there as a kid?"

"A Birthday poser," Whitton said. "Very intriguing, but right now we'd better head out and see if we can do some real detective work."

CHAPTER THIRTY

Whitton and Smith walked inside the small conference room together. The rest of the team were already seated. Smith blushed slightly when he saw what was in the middle of the table. A decent-sized chocolate cake with icing on the top had been placed there. A lone candle stood in the middle of it.

"We couldn't find room for enough candles," Bridge spoke first. "Happy birthday, mate."

The rest of the team said their happy birthdays and then Brownhill coughed to indicate it was time to get down to business.

"Right," the DI began. "Let's make a start. We have a couple of new developments to go through, and then I suggest we put our heads together and see if we can come up with something to move this investigation forwards. As you're all aware, Superintendent Smyth has invited a few of our esteemed friends from the press along to his crime stats presentation tomorrow, and I'm sure you'll all agree it would be good to be able to give them something positive."

"Stupid fool," Bridge said under his breath.

"That may be true," Brownhill had obviously heard him. "But we need to work quickly on this."

"You mentioned new developments," Smith reminded her. "What might they be?"

"Grant's IT expert has finished with Taylor Fox's laptop. What he found was mostly study related, but he did come across something interesting. An appointment diary of sorts. We know already that Miss Fox had scheduled a meeting with the head of the law faculty on Wednesday at 5pm, an appointment we also know she didn't keep. But there was another meeting pencilled in for an hour earlier that same day."

"Who was she due to meet?" Smith asked.

"Unfortunately, that part is rather cryptic. All it said in the diary was PS – 31.1 16.00."

"Thirty-first January, 4pm," Yang Chu stated the obvious. "But what does the PS stand for?"

"I'm afraid I have no idea," Brownhill admitted. "Any thoughts?"

"Whatever it stands for almost certainly has something to do with her death," Smith said.

"I agree," Whitton said. "Taylor Fox was last seen at around three on Wednesday. If she had a meeting with someone at four, it's quite reasonable to assume whoever she was meeting is also the person who killed her."

"Let's not assume anything here," Brownhill warned. "Until we figure out what this PS stands for, we still have nothing."

"Then we ask around," Smith suggested. "Maybe it's new-student-speak for something. Maybe it's a common abbreviation in this modern student-infested cess pit we call York."

"You really don't like students, do you?" Bridge laughed.

"That's enough," Brownhill said. "It's worth a shot. We'll ask around and see if anybody knows what it means."

"What's the other development?" Smith asked. "You said there were a couple."

"It's confirmed that the third victim, Rene Downs was injected with Flunitrazepam. The same as the other two. Dr Bean discovered a needle mark on the back of her thigh and there were large amounts of the drug in what little blood was left inside her."

"But we knew that already, didn't we?" Smith said. "Whoever did this injected her at home, waited for the drug to take affect and then performed a blood transfusion."

"Dr Bean's report also suggests that Miss Downs knew her attacker. There was nothing found to suggest she put up any kind of a struggle. No defence wounds, and no traces of skin or blood under her fingernails. It appears that whoever did this simply gained access to her flat and once inside, injected her and drained her blood."

"I think I've come up with a motive," Smith had decided now was a good time to broach the subject of art. "Please hear me out. I realise this may sound a bit far-fetched, but I was up most of the night researching and I think I could be onto something."

"Go on," Brownhill said.

"Art," Smith said simply. "I believe our killer is using the blood he's taken as a form of paint in his art."

"I think you need more sleep," Bridge said. "Who in their right mind would use blood to paint with?"

"Quite a few people as it turns out," Smith educated him. "Like I said, I've done some extensive research and this art form is actually quite popular."

"No," Bridge was adamant. "That's probably the maddest hypothesis I've ever heard you suggest. Painting in blood? Whatever next?"

"It makes sense. It turns out that blood isn't an easy thing to paint with due to its tendency to dry very quickly. Some of the artists I read about claimed to have used five to six litres on a single medium-sized canvas to finish off the painting. It needs to be layered, and care must be taken not to expose too much of it to the air at any one time."

"I still think we're barking up the wrong tree," Bridge said.

"Are there any other trees you suggest we start barking up? This is a worthwhile lead and it needs to be investigated."

"Do you have any suggestions as to where we can start looking?" Brownhill joined in.

"I do, as a matter of fact. The previous head of pathology. Dr Dessai."

"And what makes you think she can help?"

Smith glanced across at Whitton before replying. His wife smiled and offered a slight nod.

"Not only is Dr Dessai an expert in all things blood and guts," Smith said. "She also happens to paint in her spare time."

Add that to the fact that she was once caught red-handed stealing blood from the lab to use in her painting, and she's the ideal woman to bring in for questioning, Smith thought but kept quiet.

"What harm can it do?" he added.

"No harm at all," Brownhill decided. "Find out when Dr Dessai is available to talk and go and see her. Does anybody have anything else to add?"

Nobody did. Smith's suggestion of a motive had silenced the whole room.

"Let's get started then," Brownhill said. "Smith, you and Whitton can start with Dr Dessai. Bridge, I want you and Yang Chu to do some digging at the University again. Find out if anyone can shed any light on what PS might be an abbreviation of. I've got a meeting with the press liaison officer, the DCI and Superintendent Smyth regarding tomorrow's press conference. Smith, you are no longer needed in that meeting. We'll meet back here for another briefing at three. Now, if there's nothing further."

"Just one thing, boss," Smith glanced at the chocolate cake in the middle of the table. "Whose idea was that?"

"PC Baldwin thought it would be a good idea."

"It was," Smith said. "I'll make sure to thank her on the way out. Did I mention Whitton's organised a do at the Hog's Head for my birthday this evening?"

"Once or twice," Brownhill said.

"6pm. You're all welcome."

CHAPTER THIRTY ONE

Dr Dessai had agreed to meet Smith and Whitton in her office at the hospital. The former head of the pathology department hadn't asked what they wanted to talk to them about and Smith hadn't elaborated. "I just need to speak to Kenny first," Smith told Whitton. "He needs to be kept in the loop about this."

If Smith was expecting an objection from his wife, it didn't materialise. Whitton nodded. "I'll grab some coffee from the canteen. Come and get me when you're finished."

Dr Kenny Bean looked fresh-faced when Smith went inside his office. Considering the amount of Ireland's best, he'd consumed the previous day, he had colour in his face and his eyes were bright.

"How do you do it?" Smith asked by way of a hello. "If I'd drunk all that Guinness I'd look like shit."

"Stout is a different kettle of fish to beer," Kenny gestured for Smith to sit down. "It's more like food in liquid form. What can I do for you?"

Smith sat opposite him. He wasn't sure where to begin. "I came here out of courtesy. And before I say anything, you must understand that I am only doing my job."

"Am I under arrest?"

"Of course not. I've arranged to speak to Dr Dessai about painting with blood. I'm afraid I'm obliged to follow up on the information you gave me. And she will no doubt realise this information came from you."

"I see."

"She is not a suspect," Smith continued. "What I really want is some insight into the art form, and as she not only knows about art, but is an expert on anatomy we need to speak to her."

"I expected as much."

"I know you told me everything in confidence, but I had no choice. What did you say?"

Kenny Bean had a smile on his face. "I expected as much. And I would have been disappointed if you didn't want to speak to Rani about it."

"So, you're not pissed off?"

"Of course not. Rani and I are never going to be close again. I've accepted that. And she's hardly going to want the fact that she was caught stealing blood to be public knowledge, so you have my blessing. Although you would have spoken to her anyway, wouldn't you? With or without my blessing."

"Probably," Smith admitted. "Thanks, Kenny. That was easier than I thought it would be."

"Can I ask you something?"

"Of course."

"*Are* you treating Rani as a suspect?"

"I'm a police detective," Smith replied. "I treat everyone as a suspect until I'm convinced otherwise. And that will probably be the case with Dr Dessai. Thanks again, Kenny. And don't forget the thing for my birthday this evening. Hog's Head. 6pm."

"I'll see you there, and happy birthday."

Smith found Whitton in the small gift shop in the hospital reception area.

"Were you looking for a present for my birthday?" he asked her from behind.

Whitton jumped and turned around. "Don't creep up on people like that. Of course not – these places are just full of flowers, chocolates and fluffy things. Is Dr Bean okay with us talking to Dr Dessai?"

"It went much better than I expected. Come on – Dr Dessai's office is just down the corridor."

Smith knocked on the door and waited. Soon afterwards the door opened and a very suspicious-looking Dr Dessai stood in the doorway. She looked past Smith and Whitton down the corridor.

"Come in. And please close the door."

Dr Dessai had been transferred to the Endoscopy department after the incident with the blood. The department was small, and both Dr Bean and Dr Dessai had agreed that, although it was a small drop on the pay scale, it was far more attractive than the alternative.

"Please take a seat," Dr Dessai said. "What is this all about?"

Smith and Whitton sat on two surprisingly comfortable armchairs opposite the doctor's desk.

"We're actually here for your advice," Smith had rehearsed what he was going to say in advance. "Advice on two things actually."

"Advice on what exactly?"

"Dr Dessai, we know exactly why you were transferred here from Pathology."

"How?" she glared at Smith. "Only..."

The penny seemed to drop.

"Dr Bean told me in the strictest confidence," Smith told her. "And I am not planning on betraying that confidence. You have my word."

"Then what is it you want?"

"Like my colleague said," Whitton said. "We need your advice."

"About blood and art," Smith came out with it.

"What do you need to know?"

"I've done some research, and it appears that using human blood in painting is nothing new. What I'm trying to understand is why. Why would someone want to do such a thing? What's wrong with ordinary paint?"

"That's a good question," Dr Dessai said. "And believe me, you're not the first to ask it. Are you interested in art, detective?"

"Not really," Smith admitted.

"What about you?" the doctor addressed the question to Whitton.

"Not at all."

"Some people believe that all art is quite useless," Dr Dessai said. "And who am I to argue with them? Everyone has their own opinion and we must respect that, but to some people, myself included, when I gaze upon a painting that really grabs at my insides, it triggers emotions. It captivates me. Everyone is different, and as such, we don't all have the same tastes. As a woman of science, I understand more than most what happens in the human body when an external pleasure source triggers internal chemicals."

Smith and Whitton listened intently. Dr Dessai was becoming quite animated.

"It starts in the brain," she continued on. "The external stimulus releases chemicals such as endorphins. Feel-good chemicals. Certain art does that to me. Some people drink alcohol, some people take drugs to trigger these same chemicals. I do not, but I don't judge. Like I said, we are all different. There are people who bungee jump to get an adrenaline rush. Others like to jump out of perfectly functioning planes. They all do it to achieve the same end. To feel good. There is no way in a million years you will get me jumping out of an aeroplane, yet quite a few people do it again and again."

"You and me both, doctor," Smith said. "Me and planes don't seem to get along. But you haven't answered my question. Why use human blood to paint with?"

"Because it's alive I suppose. Or at least it once was. The cells are dead, but what was once rushing through a warm body now lives on and on, on a canvas."

"What about you?" Whitton said. "Why did you paint with blood?"

Dr Dessai appeared unsure of how to answer the question. She rubbed her nose and turned to look at a diagram of the human anatomy on the wall.

"It was an experiment," she said eventually. "That's all. A simple experiment. And to be honest, the end result was rather disappointing. Give me oil paint any day."

"Do you have any photos of your paintings?" Smith asked. "The ones you painted with blood?"

"No. And I destroyed them all. Like I said, they didn't turn out as I'd have liked them to."

"Thank you for your time, Dr Dessai," Smith said. "We won't take up any more of it."

"Can I ask you a question?" the doctor said.

"Of course."

"What we've spoken about today – all this talk of human blood and art, does it have anything to do with the students who were killed?"

"As I said, we won't take up any more of your time."

"I'll take that as a yes then. I may work on the other side of the hospital to the pathology department, detective, but I still hear about what goes on. Those young women all had their blood removed, didn't they? Do you believe that blood was used in art?"

"It is a theory we're looking into," Smith admitted.

"Hmm. Three young women. They were all drugged, weren't they?"

"You certainly do hear about what goes on," Smith said.

"Their deaths weren't at all violent," she ignored his flippancy. "Death was just a by-product – it was the blood that was important, and whoever did this didn't want them to suffer."
Smith hadn't thought about this, and it made him angry with himself. Dr Dessai had hit the nail on the head. They weren't looking for some crazed psychopath who kills women for their blood – they were looking for a very controlled individual who has so far planned everything meticulously, and his new theory about the motive was looking more and more promising.

CHAPTER THIRTY TWO

"Where do we even start looking?" Yang Chu asked Bridge outside the impressive looking University Library.

The snow clouds from the previous day had drifted off, the sky was clear and there was now a crisp chill in the air.

Bridge buttoned up his coat. "I reckon the library is as good a place to start as anywhere else."

They went inside and Bridge looked around. In front of one of the walls was a long counter. Two tired-looking young women were sitting there. Both of them were looking at mobile phones.

"Let's ask over there," he said to Yang Chu.

"Excuse me," he said to one of the women. "Are you a student here?"

She looked up from her phone and rolled her eyes. "I was, but now I have the pleasure of replying to mundane questions all day long. Lucky me."

"You were about to say *how can I help you?*" Bridge wasn't put off by her surly demeanour. "I can tell. It was on the tip of your tongue, wasn't it?"

The woman's features softened slightly, but she still didn't smile.

"Go on," Bridge urged. "*How can I help you?*"

The woman sitting next to her did smile. Bridge saw from the badge on her jacket that her name was Lisa Fry.

"How can I help you?" she obliged.

"Detective Sergeant Bridge," he still swelled with pride when he said his rank out loud. "And this is DC Yang Chu. Lisa, we're investigating the murders of the three students here."

"It's awful," Lisa said. "Nobody feels safe anymore."

"Did you know any of the women who were killed?" Yang Chu asked.

"I knew Taylor," she replied. "Not very well. We did a couple of the same modules."

Bridge thought hard. "Are you studying Business Studies too?"

"Psychology."

"I thought Taylor Fox was doing a Business Studies degree," Bridge said.

"Things are different now. It's much more flexible than before. I'm reading Psychology, but I can do a French module if I want to expand my horizons."

"So, Taylor Fox was in some of your Psychology classes?" Yang Chu said.

This was news to them. They knew about Taylor's interest in business law, but not Psychology.

"I suppose business and psychology can make quite a useful combination," Lisa said. "Are you getting any closer to catching who did this? We're all terrified to go out at night."

"We're working on some new leads," Bridge didn't want to elaborate on Smith's new macabre motive theory. "Is there somewhere we can talk in private?"

"We're not exactly run off our feet at the moment," the dour woman sitting next to Lisa said.

Bridge had actually forgotten she was even there.

"We can go to the coffee bar around the corner," Lisa suggested.

"What's with your friend in the library?" Bridge asked Lisa and placed three coffees on the table. "She must be a real pleasure to work with."

"Sandy's alright," Lisa said. "She's just not really a Monday person. And she doesn't particularly like her job."

"Does she work in the library full time then?" Yang Chu asked.

"She's bitter because that's about all she could get when she finished her degree. Second class degrees in English Lit are not exactly well sought after from employers."

"And you're reading Psychology?" Bridge said. "Is that right?"

"I've always been fascinated with what makes us tick," Lisa said and blushed slightly. "I suppose that's a real Psych cliché isn't it?"

"Not at all," Bridge smiled at her. "I completely agree with you."

Yang Chu glared at him. If he was a betting man, he'd stake his life savings on Bridge asking her for her phone number when they were finished.

"This probably sounds a bit weird," Bridge said. "I'm not long out of Uni myself but things seem to have changed quite a bit since I was here. I was wondering if there is such a thing as student speak. University jargon. Abbreviations, that sort of thing."

"I'm not sure what you mean," Lisa said.

"Shortened versions of stuff," Yang Chu explained rather inelegantly. "Like text-speak."

"IT," Bridge gave an example. "Do you abbreviate your classes?"

"Oh, you mean that," Lisa suddenly understood what they were talking about. "We do shorten the titles of the modules."

"Do you have any idea what PS might be short for?" Yang Chu asked.

"PS?" Lisa repeated. "It doesn't ring any bells."

"Could the P stand for Psychology?" Bridge suggested.

"Possibly, but I can't think what the S could mean. Are you sure it's not just PS as in postscript?"

"We don't think so," Bridge thought back to what was written in Taylor Fox's diary and *postscript* just didn't fit in that context.

"I'd better be getting back to the library," Lisa said. "I'm sorry I couldn't be of any help."

"No," Bridge said. "You've been a great help. If you do think of what PS might mean give me a call any time."

He gave her one of his cards, and added, "my mobile number's on there too so you can reach me after hours."

Yang Chu groaned inwardly. He was seriously contemplating taking up gambling.

CHAPTER THIRTY THREE

Whitton's phone started to ring the moment Smith turned the key in the ignition in the car park at the hospital.

She looked at the screen. "It's Laura's day-care."

She pressed *answer*, and Smith waited before he drove out of the car park. Whitton did more listening than talking and from the expression on her face Smith could tell that something was wrong.

"Laura's been sick," Whitton told him when she'd ended the call. "She's been throwing up all morning. They think it's some stomach bug that's been going round. They think we should come and fetch her."

"She was fine this morning," Smith said. "Bloody day-care. All they seem to do there is breed bacteria."

"It's unavoidable," Whitton defended. "And it's also what builds up their immune systems."

"Let's go and get her then," Smith wasn't happy at all.

Ever since placing Laura in day-care, not a week had gone by without her coming home with some bug or other. He knew deep down that Whitton was right – it was how children's immune systems strengthened, but it was still annoying.

"I'll go and fetch her," Whitton offered. "Our house is on the way anyway. I'll pick up my car and you can head back to the station."

"Are you sure?"

"It's senseless both of us taking time off work," Whitton said. "Especially in the middle of the investigation."

"Phone me if you need me," Smith said. "I let Brownhill know what's going on."

They drove in silence the whole way home. Smith dropped Whitton off and watched her go inside the house to get her car keys. He drove off without waiting for her emerge from the house again. His phone beeped to tell him he'd received a message. He took it out of his pocket and opened up the screen. The message was from Jessica Blakemore and it was very brief. It consisted of a simple '*I may have something*' and an address. Smith was about to write a reply when a loud hooting noise made him look up. While he was looking at the screen on the mobile phone he'd drifted onto the other side of the road and a large truck was racing towards him. He quickly swerved back onto the left-hand side of the road. He narrowly missed the oncoming truck and he received a less-than-polite hand signal from the driver. "Shit," he pulled over in the car park of a supermarket to try and slow his heartbeat. It was cold in the car, but beads of sweat had formed on his forehead. He made a mental note to never look at his phone while driving again. A few more seconds and Laura would have had to grow up without a father. Whitton would be a widow.

After a few minutes, Smith felt composed enough to set off on the road again. His phone was safely tucked away in his coat pocket. He'd memorised Jessica Blakemore's address. He knew the area well. It was in a housing estate just outside the city that had been built around ten years earlier. He stopped his car outside the house and looked around. The estate still looked very new – identical two-up two-down semi-detached houses stood in neat rows, and small, well-kept gardens stood in front. Smith walked the short distance to the front door and knocked. He couldn't find a doorbell. When nobody answered he knocked again.

Still no answer.

He could hear music coming from somewhere. He took out his phone and realised he hadn't sent the message he intended to send to Jessica Blakemore informing her he was on his way. The near-death experience had side-tracked him. He called her number, but it went straight to voicemail. He tried the door handle. The door was open.

The smell hit Smith's nostrils as soon as he entered the house. It was a pungent smell, and a very familiar one at that. A thick, warm stench with a metallic edge to it. The music he'd heard earlier was louder inside the house. It was coming from upstairs. He walked down the hallway and the odour become more noticeable. There was a strange sizzling sound coming from the kitchen. Smith went in the kitchen and stopped next to a black worktop. On it was a white chopping board that was now stained red. A very sharp knife was lying on top of it, the blade covered in what looked like small, thick globules of dark flesh.

The source of the stench was in a small frying pan on top of a gas cooker. The gas was turned down low and inside the frying pan were chopped up pieces of reddish-brown matter that were slowly turning grey. The smell was making Smith feel sick.

"Don't you believe in knocking?" a voice behind him made his heart stop for a few beats.

He turned around. Jessica Blakemore was standing behind him. She was dressed in a pair of tracksuit pants and a checked shirt that was at least two sizes too big for her.

"I did knock," Smith told her. "Twice. And I tried to call but it went straight to voicemail. What on earth is that smell?"

"It stinks, doesn't it?" Jessica made a face like a grimace. "It's liver. Pete likes it slow-fried. He loves it, so I put up with the smell. It's worth it just to see the look on his face when he eats it."

"Pete?"

The owner of the large checked shirt, Smith thought.

"He's the only man in my life," Jessica said with a theatrical shake of the head.

"I see," Smith said.

"He stands about a foot off the ground and he's covered in fur. He's a Ginger Tom."

"A cat?"

"I can see why they made you detective sergeant. He doesn't live here. He turned up just after I moved in. I think he's a stray. But he loves his liver. It should be just about done."

Smith watched as she turned off the gas and moved the unappetising looking pieces of grey offal around in the pan.

"Where were we?" Jessica said.

"I did knock," Smith said once more.

"I was busy upstairs," Jessica said. "I had some music playing. You could have phoned first to let me know you were coming."

"I was in the middle of replying to your message when a large truck took a bit of a dislike to me. It missed me by inches and I sort of lost my train of thought after that. What did you mean when you said you might have something?"

"Oh that. It could be nothing, but I thought of something. I tried to think of all kinds of reasons why a person would remove the blood from someone after killing them, but I couldn't think of anything apart from ritualistic blood-drinking and cult activity."

"We've explored those avenues," Smith told her.

"And it doesn't fit. Drinking blood is extremely dangerous. You can actually overdose on blood due to its rich iron content. And cult activity consists of, in ninety-nine percent of cases, nut jobs who simply wouldn't have it in them to kill anything more than a house sparrow. No, this is something totally different. What we are looking at here is a psychotic individual. But not all the time."

"What do you mean by that?"

"When the murders were carried out, from the information you've given me, this looks like a perfectly calm and collected individual. Nothing was left to chance. The locations were carefully selected as were the victims. The method of killing was more gentle than malicious, and the deaths were mere by-products of the end goal."

"You're the second person to say that this morning," Smith said. "That the deaths were mere by-products. But it still doesn't tell us anything more than we already know."

"Then stop interrupting me and listen. The goal of this killer is blood. Lots of blood. If we do some crude arithmetic, we can say we're looking at around twenty-five to thirty pints of blood. Your killer is almost definitely someone with medical knowledge, and I'm eighty percent certain it's a woman."

"What makes you so sure?"

"It's not so simple to carry out a blood transfusion," Jessica said. "And to extract the quantities in question requires skill. As to the sex of the murderer, the method of killing is gentle, caring even and that strikes me as the way a woman would kill. And before you ask me why I believe so much blood was taken, that's where the psychosis comes in. After calmly killing these women and extracting their blood, I believe the killer is halfway to the goal. There is now no need to be careful – the risky part is over and the main objective can begin."

"And what is the main objective?"

"Creativity. Absolute creativity. There are no boundaries and the artist can use what was once alive to create something immortal."

CHAPTER THIRTY FOUR

"It looks like I was spot on with this art thing," Smith told Bridge about what both Dr Dessai and Jessica Blakemore had said.

Smith, Bridge and Yang Chu were sitting in the canteen, drinking coffee before the three o'clock briefing.

"Two very different people said exactly the same thing. That cannot be just a coincidence."

"You hate coincidences," Bridge reminded Smith of one of his favourite mantras.

"Two well-educated people speaking the exact same words is enough for me," Smith continued. "That's more than enough for me."

"Where's Whitton?" Yang Chu changed the subject.

"Laura isn't very well," Smith said and realised he hadn't called Whitton to find out how his daughter was. "The day-care phoned and said she'd been throwing up all morning. That place is a haven for bugs."

"I'm never having kids," Bridge said. "They seem to be nothing but trouble."

"Probably for the best," Smith mused and walked over to the window to phone his wife.

He brought up her number, pressed *dial*, and almost immediately heard the cringe-worthy introduction to Meat Loaf's *Bat out of Hell* coming up the stairs.

Whitton walked in and Smith ended the call.

"How's Laura doing?" he asked her. "I was calling you."

"I know," Whitton put her phone back in her pocket. "She seemed to make a remarkable recovery as soon as she got home. My parents are looking after her. I didn't want to leave the team short-handed."

"Do you want some coffee?" Smith offered.

"I've not long finished one at my parent's house. Anything new come up?"

Smith told her about his interesting meeting with Jessica Blakemore.

"I don't believe you went to see her again," Whitton said when he'd finished. "I thought you'd have learned your lesson by now."

"She called me," Smith said. "And she said exactly the same thing as Dr Dessai. Don't you think that's significant?"

"Let me see. A nut-job who's spent the best part of the past six years in a madhouse, and a doctor who was caught stealing blood to paint with agree on something. I'd say they'd make a sterling job in the witness box. Quite a double act. The judge and jury would take them very seriously, I'm sure."

"Sarcasm doesn't suit you, Erica."

"Listen to yourself. You're so obsessed with the idea that this psycho is killing women so he can use their blood to create art, that you'll believe anything as long as it supports your crazy theory."

"She," Smith corrected her. "We're looking at a woman here. And it's not a crazy theory. It's been backed up."

"By a self-confessed mad woman and a blood thief," Whitton reminded him.

"Maybe it takes a mad woman to get inside the head of another mad woman," Smith countered. "I asked your so-called nut-job to my birthday thing at the Hog's Head this evening by the way."

"You did what?"

"She's a good friend. Whether you like it or not, Jessica is a good friend of mine."

Whitton was about to say something when she was stopped short.

"I thought I would find you in here." It was DI Brownhill. "The briefing was supposed to start ten minutes ago."

"Before we begin," Brownhill said in the small conference room. "I'll outline what was discussed in the meeting pertaining to tomorrow's press conference. Neil Walker has decided that it would be imprudent to mention too many details about the recent murders. In the interests of panic amongst the general public, the fact that all three women had their blood removed is not to be disclosed."

"Can I say something, boss?" Smith said.

"Of course."

"Can we please speak in plain English in here? You're not talking to the press now."

"Point taken," Brownhill said. "DCI Chalmers agrees with the press liaison officer's recommendations."

"What about old Smyth?" Smith asked.

"The Superintendent didn't appear to have an opinion either way," Brownhill sighed. "He was more focused on his crime statistics. He did wonder if it would be at all possible for this sorry mess to be cleared up before the presentation tomorrow evening."

"His words," Smith and Bridge said in unison.

"His words," Brownhill confirmed. "Apparently three unsolved murders are not going to look too good for his stats. Now, can we press on with more important matters? Bridge, did you find anything new at the University?"

"Business law wasn't the only extra module Taylor Fox was taking," Bridge began. "We spoke with one of the students doing a Psychology degree and she mentioned that Miss Fox was in some of the same classes. It appears she liked to keep her options open."

"What about the acronym?" Brownhill said. "PS. Do we know what the letters stand for?"

"I'm afraid not, Ma'am. The P could be for Psychology but the student we spoke to couldn't say what the S meant."

"Psychology is a start. We'll come back to that. Smith, how did the meeting with Dr Dessai pan out? I hope you were discreet."

"Discreet is my middle name, boss," Smith said.

Whitton exhaled a very indiscreet sigh.

"Dr Dessai was very gracious about the whole thing," Smith carried on, unperturbed. "It appears she's moved on and forgotten about the incident. She did give us some interesting insight into where we can carry on looking. It does appear that this is all connected somehow with art. And some of the things she mentioned together with another conversation I had today made me realise we are not looking at an out-of control individual here, this killer is exceptionally calm and collected. Probably well-educated and not somebody you would pin the label, *murderer* on when you first meet them."

"You mentioned another conversation," Brownhill said. "Who were you talking to?"

"Jessica Blakemore," Whitton scoffed before Smith had a chance to answer.

"You went to see her again?" Brownhill's eyes darkened. "Do you not recall the previous conversation we had on this subject?"

"She called me, boss," Smith explained. "She said she'd thought of something useful and it turns out she was right. She agreed totally with Dr Dessai's take on this killer and she gave me even more. This is all to do with art. The blood from these women is taken to paint with. The artist goes through stages. The first is the planning stage where the location of the murder and the intended victim are selected. Then it's the murder itself. These two stages are carefully planned, and nothing is left to chance. The final stage is the one where the artist can finally let go. There are no boundaries, now – the sky's the limit. The materials ready to be put to use on the canvas have come at a price, but the end-result is worth it."

The room was quiet. Smith's little soliloquy had silenced the whole team.

"Hold on," Bridge was the first to speak. "What did you say about boundaries?"

"There are no boundaries," Smith said.

"I've heard that before sometime this week."

"It was that art student from the University," Yang Chu reminded him.

"The career student. The first victim's boyfriend. He said something about going through a phase of experimental art where he could push the boundaries. He mentioned some of the artists who'd tried. Castiglia and Frank Bacon I think they were called."

"Francis Bacon," Smith recalled some of the gruesome images from the previous night. "Vincent Castiglia and Francis Bacon both painted with human blood. I remember them from the research I did last night."

"We have a suspect at last," Brownhill said.

"No, we don't, boss," Smith had remembered something else. Something the head of the law faculty had said when Smith asked him about the landscapes he painted and their unusual colours.

The paint I use is very costly.

"We've got two," Smith said. "We now have two very viable suspects."

CHAPTER THIRTY FIVE

The artist watched the sun disappear behind the city in the distance. The spires of the Minster turned from orange to dark red and then black. Lights were being turned on in the houses in the foreground and darkness quickly descended over the people of York. For one of York's temporary residents this would be the last sunset they ever see and by tomorrow the student population would be fewer in number by one. *This can't go on*, the artist thought. *This can't possibly go on.*

With the curtains closed, the artist scrutinised the scene on the canvas in the corner. Much larger and bolder than the others, this one would be hard to outshine. But it was possible – it could be done.

A loud shriek from the street below woke the artist from the visions that were already forming.

Two cats were fighting in the dusk half-light and one of them was clearly getting the better of the other. The piercing noise ended with one final crescendo and then the only sound from the street was the odd car passing by.

The artist stood in the doorway, cast one final glance at the most recent piece and, suitably inspired walked down the stairs and left the house. There was blood on the wall next to the house. No doubt the result of the catfight. The artist stared at it for some time and wondered who had come off victorious this time. The finger seemed to work independently from the brain as it pressed against the scene of the battle. The blood was still warm, yet a thin skin was already forming on the surface. A car approached and the artist turned away from the blinding headlights.

CHAPTER THIRTY SIX

Greg Walsh clearly wasn't pleased to see Smith and Yang Chu standing on his doorstep. The career student glared at both of them. He was wearing a large white shirt that was smattered with paint of all colours.

"What do you want?" he said, and Smith could smell the alcohol on his breath immediately.

"Mr Walsh," Smith said. "Can we come inside?"

"Do I have a choice?"

"You do, actually," Smith told him. "But I'd prefer it if you let us in. There are some questions we need to ask you, and I'd really like to have a look at some of your art. Especially your more recent work."

"What is this all about? What has my art got to do with anything?"

"He's a bit of an art buff," Yang Chu lied. "Could you please step aside and let us in?"

"I won't offer you anything to drink, if that's alright," Greg said in the living room. "And could you please make this quick. I was actually in the middle of something."

"A painting?" Smith asked.

"That's right."

"Can we have a look?"

"I thought you were an art buff," Greg scoffed. "Then you ought to know that no artist likes to display a work in progress."

Smith stood up. "I believe you use your spare room as a studio. I'm sure I'll find it."

Greg shot up out of his seat and stood in the doorway. "I don't want you to go up there. Do you even have a warrant? You can't just barge in here and search my house. I think I should call my lawyer."

"Go ahead," Smith had heard this sort of veiled threat many times before. "And while you're waiting, I'll just have a quick look at your paintings. Please get out of my way."

Greg Walsh seemed to be considering his options. He looked at Smith and then at Yang Chu. His eyes darted from side to side.

"Why do you want to see my art?" he said eventually. "Why is it so important to look at my paintings?"

"I'll let you know when I've had a look," Smith barged past him and headed up the stairs.

Greg Walsh's studio was situated in a small bedroom that looked out onto the back yard. The smell inside the room was overpowering. It was a chemical smell that burned the inside of the nostrils. Another smell still lingered in the air. It was a smell Smith was very familiar with – a pungent peppery odour. In an ashtray on a table next to the window was a thick half-smoked rolled-up cigarette. Next to it was an empty bottle of red wine and a wine glass. Finished paintings were propped up against the wall. All of them were landscapes, and most of them were painted in the same reddish-brown colour. There was a large easel on the floor. On it was a canvas that was covered in a white sheet. Smith approached it and placed his hand on the sheet.

"It's not finished yet," Greg appeared in the doorway.

Yang Chu was standing behind him.

"Can you smell something illegal?" he said to Smith.

"It's in the ashtray," Smith said.

"It helps me to free my mind," Greg Walsh explained. "I don't deal – I just smoke a bit every now and then."

"We're not interested in a bit of weed," Smith said.

It wasn't that long ago since he'd stopped smoking marijuana himself.

"But we are interested in what's behind that sheet," he added.

"Please," Greg begged. "Please don't touch it."

Smith turned around. "I won't damage it. I just want to have a look."

"Please," Greg pleaded. "I don't like people seeing my art before it's finished."

Smith ignored him. With one swift tug, he removed the sheet and uncovered the painting.

Greg Walsh was right – the piece of art on the canvas in front of Smith was clearly far from finished. But it was still clear what the painting consisted of. This one was definitely not a landscape. The background was dark blue, and it formed a sharp contrast to the main subject of the painting. On a chair in the centre of the picture was a woman dressed all in white. Her features were not quite defined yet, but they were clear enough for Smith to see a definite likeness of somebody he recognised. He had to admit that Greg Walsh really was very good. The woman on the chair was clearly Kirsty King – the twenty-year-old law student who was found a few days ago with all of the blood drained from her body.

Smith turned and looked Greg in the eyes. "And what are we supposed to make of that painting?"

"It's Kirsty," Greg said.

"I know exactly who it is. What I want to know is why you're painting a woman who was murdered last week."

Greg looked like he was about to pass out. The colour had drained from his face and his hands were shaking.

"It's my way of dealing with it," he said in a voice no more than a whisper. "I loved Kirsty. I can't stop thinking about what happened to her – how she died, and the painting is a way of remembering her how she really was."

Smith looked at Yang Chu. "Get hold of Webber. I want a team here within the hour. I want every inch of this place searched. And I want every painting in this room checked."

Yang Chu took out his phone and went back downstairs.

Smith turned to Greg Walsh. "I think it's time you got hold of that lawyer you spoke about earlier."

CHAPTER THIRTY SEVEN

Whitton and Bridge were up against a much trickier opponent in Henry Dewbury. The Doctor of Law had not only used his right to refuse them entry to his property without a search warrant, he'd also used his right to remain silent. Bridge didn't know what to do. In the end he'd resorted to calling Brownhill and the DI had instructed them to arrest Dr Dewbury and bring him in for questioning.

"You are making a huge mistake," Henry Dewbury said when Bridge had finished cautioning him. "A huge mistake. Reasonable grounds for arrest. Do those words mean anything to you? I suggest you reconsider and think about exactly who you're dealing with here." "I suggest you exercise that right to remain silent until we get to the station," Whitton was getting sick of the sound of his voice. "Could you do that for us, please?"

Henry Dewbury spent the whole journey to the police station on his mobile phone, arranging for a colleague of his to meet him there, and by the time Bridge stopped in the car park, Whitton had a throbbing headache.

"Please come with us," Bridge instructed their suspect. "We'll get the ball rolling."

"You're going to regret this," Henry Dewbury remained defiant. "You will see how powerful the law actually is after this. You mark my words."

Whitton was glad to see Brownhill by the front desk when they walked in.

The DI nodded to Henry Dewbury. "The custody officer will be with you shortly. Please take a seat."

"You're making a big mistake," Henry told her. "You have no grounds for arrest here."

"You refused my officers entry to your property, Dr Dewbury," Brownhill said. "You also refused to answer any questions put to you, and that tends to arouse suspicion. You will be held here until we are satisfied that suspicion is unfounded. Now, please take a seat. I assume you have arranged legal representation."

For once, Henry Dewbury was speechless. The DI's words had silenced him. He shook his head and sat down opposite the front desk.

* * *

"Interview with Gregory Walsh commenced 16.00," Smith began. "Present, DS Smith and DC Yang Chu. For the record, Mr Walsh has declined legal representation. Mr Walsh, do you understand why you were arrested?"

"I didn't kill anybody," Greg said. "I had nothing to do with what happened to Kirsty."

"Mr Walsh," Smith said. "I'd like to go back to Saturday 28th January. Can you remember where you were on that day?"

"I already told him," Greg pointed to Yang Chu.

"For the tape, please."

Greg scratched his nose. "I met up with Kirsty for coffee."

"You're referring to Kirsty King?" Smith said.

"That's right."

"What time was this?"

"Around lunchtime."

"Could you be a bit more specific," Yang Chu said.

"It was around noon. We had a chat and a coffee at a place near the halls of residence."

"Can anybody confirm this?" Smith asked.

"Probably. I don't know. I don't make a habit of making sure I have a watertight alibi every time I go out."

"Calm down, Mr Walsh," Smith said. "So, you had coffee with Miss King. Then what?"

"Then she left."

"What time was this?"

"It was after a couple of hours."

"So around two then?"

"Right. Then I went to the Trout for a few beers."

"The Trout is a student pub," Yang Chu informed Smith.

"And Miss King," Smith said. "Do you know where she went after she left the coffee shop?"

"She said she was going home – she had a project she needed to work on, so she went home."

"OK," Smith decided to try another approach. "We found a recent painting of Kirsty King in your studio earlier. Could you explain that?"

"There's nothing to explain. I told you – it's a way of dealing with things. Art is a great healer if that makes any sense. I didn't kill Kirsty. I didn't kill any of those women. I'm an art student – I'm not a murderer. How long do I have to stay in here?"

"Until we're finished. Are you aware of the artists, Vincent Castiglia and Francis Bacon?"

"Of course," Greg frowned. "They're brilliant artists."

"And are you also aware of some of their rather unorthodox painting methods?"

"Art is not an orthodox form. There are no real rules. Castiglia and Bacon have proved that."

"So, you're aware that these artists have used human blood in their work?"

"They're not the only ones. Human blood has been used by a lot of artists."

"What about you?" Yang Chu said. "Have you ever used human blood to paint with?"

"Of course not. Where would I... Is that what this is all about? You think I killed Kirsty because I wanted to use her blood?"

There was a knock on the door and PC Baldwin came in. Her eyes were wide, and she was breathing heavily.

"Can I have a word, sir?" she said to Smith.

"We're a bit busy in here," Smith told her.

"It's important."

"Interview with Gregory Walsh paused, 16:15," Smith said, paused the recording device and left the room.

"What is it, Baldwin?" Smith asked her outside.

"There's been another one, sir," Baldwin informed him. "Another student was drugged, and her blood taken."

"Shit. When was this?"

"About half an hour ago. And there's more. This time the murderer was interrupted. The woman's housemate was upstairs, and he disturbed the killer. She's still alive, sir. She's lost a lot of blood but she's still alive."

CHAPTER THIRTY EIGHT

Smith was inside the hospital within fifteen minutes. He rushed up to the front desk.

"The young woman who was brought in earlier with severe blood loss," he said to the familiar face behind the desk. "Where is she now?"

"She was taken straight to intensive care," the receptionist told him.

"Who's the doctor in charge?"

"Dr Howard."

"Thank you," Smith said and raced down the corridor.

He found Dr Howard in the waiting room outside intensive care. He was speaking with a young man next to a vending machine. He patted the man on the shoulder and walked up to Smith.

"Dr Howard," Smith had met the elderly doctor a few times before. "How's she doing?"

"Detective," Dr Howard held out a hand. "That was quick."

Smith shook his hand. "How's she doing?" he asked again.

"She's lost a lot of blood, and we're trying to get the levels back to normal again. She's on a ventilator at the moment. It was lucky her friend there found her when he did."

He nodded to the young man by the vending machine.

"How long will that take? How long until her blood starts pumping normally again?"

"We can't be too sure."

"I need to talk to her," Smith said.

"That's going to have to wait. She's suffered severe hypovolemic shock. She was unconscious when she was brought in and she's still unconscious. We're still unsure as to the extent of damage already caused. With such severe blood loss, organ failure is a distinct possibility."

"Do you think she'll be alright?"

"It's touch and go I'm afraid. She didn't have enough blood in her body for her heart to work properly - her blood pressure is still dangerously low, and until her levels are stabilised, we won't know how much damage has already been caused. I have to go. I'll keep you informed."

Smith thanked Dr Howard and got a coke from the vending machine. The young man was still standing there. He was staring blankly at the various soft drinks and chocolate bars.

"Are you alright?" Smith asked him.

"What?" the man looked like he'd been woken after having a bad dream. "Sorry, I was miles away."

"I believe you were the one who found the woman?"

"I'm Lee. Lee Wright. Haley lives in the same house as me," he said.

"Haley?"

"Haley Moore."

"Did you see who attacked her?" Smith could feel they were getting closer.

"I was in my room upstairs," Lee said. "I heard the front door, but I just assumed it was one of Haley's friends. I was about to go downstairs to make some coffee when I stood on a nail that was sticking out of the wood. I think I swore very loudly, then someone ran out of Haley's room and left the house."

"What did they look like?"

"I only saw them from behind. And whoever it was, was wearing a hooded jacket with the hood up. The door was slammed, I went to ask Haley if she wanted a coffee and that's when I saw her. I thought she was dead. Her face was an awful colour. I checked for a pulse like I've seen in the films and then I called an ambulance. They were there in minutes. Do you think she's going to be alright? She was so cold."

"It's hard to tell. This person who was in Haley's room. Is there anything you can remember about them? Height? Build? Were they carrying anything?"

"I only got a quick glance, but I'd say slim build, around five, eight. And whoever it was had a bag with them."

Smith decided to take a chance. "From what you saw, could you tell if this person was a man or a woman?"

"I couldn't be too sure. The hallway isn't very well lit – it was already dark outside, so it was even harder to see. I hope Haley is going to be alright."

"I'm sure she'll be fine," Smith said. "We'll need you to come in and make a statement, and a forensics team will need to have a look at Haley's room. Is there anybody else there at the moment?"

"John and Wendy should be back from Uni by now."

"Get hold of them and tell them what's happened. And tell them not to touch anything if possible. Someone will be around shortly."

Smith got the address from Lee Wright.

He took his coke outside and lit a cigarette. He took out his phone and made the first phone call. He called Brownhill and informed her she had the unpleasant task of telling Henry Dewbury and Greg Walsh that they were free to go. The person who attacked Haley Moore couldn't possibly be the Doctor of Law or the career student as they were both in police custody at the time. The second call was to Grant Webber. Smith told the head of forensics what had happened and gave him the address. He stubbed his cigarette out on the wall and lit another. The nicotine wasn't helping to calm his rapid heartbeat. They were getting closer – Smith could feel it. They'd just eliminated two suspects in one fell swoop, but they now had a witness. The killer had been careless this time, and Smith sensed that the mistake they'd made in leaving a victim alive would be how they would catch them.

Smith's watch told him he had just over an hour before the planned birthday gathering at the Hog's Head. He wondered if he ought to phone Marge and cancel. The recent attack on Haley Moore would require all hands on deck. He dialled Brownhill's number again.

"What now?" the DI was clearly in a foul mood.

"I was wondering where we go from here, boss," Smith said.

"Is there any news on the young woman?"

"Haley Moore. I spoke to the doctor in charge and he seems to think she's going to be unconscious for quite some time. I don't think we'll get anything out of her for a while. Doctor Howard has promised to call me if there's any change in her condition."

"Then what do you want me to tell you?"

"Is everything alright, boss?" Smith asked her.

"No, everything is not alright. I've just been on the firing end of possibly the worst abuse I've ever received. Doctor Dewbury is threatening legal action. Wrongful arrest, undue questioning, the works."

"He's just pissed off," Smith assured her. "It'll blow over. Besides, we had enough to arrest him. He'll come to realise that when he calms down. What's the plan, now?"

"Until that woman wakes up, our hands are tied. Grant is on his way to her house now, so hopefully he'll be able to give us something, but I suggest we hold tight and pray that young woman wakes up. This investigation is really becoming quite draining."

"Then you need something to take your mind off it," Smith told her. "Forget about the case for one evening – forget about old Smyth's crime stats presentation cum press conference tomorrow and join us at the Hog's Head for a few drinks. You haven't forgotten about it, have you?"

"Of course not. You could be right. It'll be a good distraction. We may be a bit late though – it depends on what time Grant finishes up at Haley Moore's house."

"See you there," Smith said and rang off.

CHAPTER THIRTY NINE

Smith, Whitton and Laura went inside the Hog's Head and Smith was immediately glad he hadn't phoned and cancelled. Marge had obviously gone to a lot of effort. Three tables had been moved together on one side of the room, and buffet food of all kinds was laid out in large platters. All three tables were covered in food. Marge emerged from the door that led to the kitchen, Smith walked up to her and flung his arms around her.

"What was that for?" Marge said when Smith had released her.

"For all this," Smith pointed to the food on the tables. "You didn't have to go to so much trouble."

"You can thank your lovely wife for that," Marge told him. "Happy birthday by the way."

"It wasn't just me," Whitton admitted. "Baldwin helped me out."

"So that was why you were being so secretive back at the station," Smith said. "I don't know what to say. Let's grab a table."

"I'll bring you some drinks over," Marge said.

Whitton's parents arrived and joined Smith and Whitton at their table. Laura had already made herself comfortable on a blanket on the floor. She was drawing something on a piece of paper. Her new-found interest in art was really keeping her busy. A waitress placed a tray of drinks on the table.

"Happy birthday, son," Harold Whitton held his pint in the air. "Here's to many more. What are we on now? Thirty-five?"

"Thirty-six," Whitton took obvious delight in telling him.

"Still a spring chicken then," Whitton's mother said.

Chalmers arrived the same time as Bridge and Baldwin. The DCI held a badly wrapped present in his hands. It was obviously a bottle of something or other.

"Mrs Chalmers was out at her Yoga class," he handed the gift to Smith. "Hence the wrapping. Happy birthday."

"Thanks boss," Smith said. "And thanks for coming."

Yang Chu walked through the door a few minutes later. There was still no sign of DI Brownhill and Grant Webber. Smith assumed Webber was still busy at Haley Moore's house. Bridge took Smith aside.

"I know it's your birthday bash and everything, but I heard about the latest victim. I believe she's still alive."

"It's touch and go," Smith told him. "The doctor promised to get in touch if there's any change."

"She must know who the killer is," Bridge continued. "We need to talk to her."

"She's unconscious, Bridge, and as you pointed out this is my birthday party, so can we leave the shop talk until we get inside the station tomorrow morning?"

"Fair enough. I haven't had a chance to get you a present yet."

"I don't want one. Just you lot being here is more than enough."

"Baldwin looks bloody gorgeous this evening," Bridge said. "I still haven't given up hope on that one."

Smith was about to say something when his attention was taken by the woman entering the pub. His wasn't the only attention being grabbed. The whole room seemed to stop what they were doing and stare at the woman with the black hair. Jessica Blakemore glanced around nervously, and her eyes finally came to rest on Smith. She was dressed in black jeans and a checked shirt. Smith walked over to her and noticed she was wearing subtle makeup. Her face didn't seem as pale as before and her eyes appeared brighter.

"Jessica," Smith placed a hand on her shoulder. "Glad you could make it. Come and join us."

"Do you think that's such a good idea?" she said. "Have you seen the way everyone is looking at me?"

"They're just curious. It's been a while and they're probably just wondering what my nut-job friend looks like now."

The ice was broken. Jessica walked with Smith back to his table.

"Good to see you again," Bridge was the first to speak.

He looked the psychiatrist up and down and smiled.

"You're looking well," he added.

The rest of the party joined in. Only Whitton kept her distance. She merely nodded to the woman her husband had invited.

"Get yourself a drink at the bar," Smith told her. "I've got a tab going."

Chalmers shot up in his chair. "Why didn't you say so before? I'll get them in then."

DI Brownhill and Grant Webber walked through the door an hour or so later. Both of them looked exhausted.

"Sorry we're late," Webber held out his hand to Smith. "The house of the latest victim took a lot longer than expected. The stupid housemates thought it would be a good idea to clean up the blood in the woman's room. I thought they'd been instructed to leave everything as it was."

"They were," Smith said, the irritation clear in his voice. "Did you manage to find anything?"

"Same MO by the looks of things. The killer got inside the house, drugged the poor woman and started the transfusion. But the killer left in a hurry this time and didn't clean up quite as well after himself. Luckily for us the housemates didn't do a very good job of cleaning up the blood. There was a shoe print on the carpet in the woman's bedroom. It's short pile so we managed to get some pretty good photographs. It's not much, but it's something. Once again, I'd say the victim knew her killer."

"She's still alive," Smith reminded him. "The murderer was interrupted this time."

"How's she doing?"

"Still unconscious. Let's just pray she wakes up. You look like you need a drink – there's a tab at the bar, and it's on me."

"In that case I'll have a double. Happy birthday by the way."

Smith remembered he'd invited Kenny Bean. The head of pathology still hadn't arrived. Smith considered phoning him to remind him but changed his mind. Dr Bean was a busy man, and maybe he couldn't get away.

The sound of a loud bell ringing was heard, and the room became silent.

"Help yourselves to the food," Marge said from behind the bar. "There's more than enough to go round so don't be shy."

"Then we want a speech," Bridge shouted. "He's not getting away with not giving a speech."

Everyone crowded around the buffet table. Smith had forgotten how greedy York's finest could be when there was free food on offer. He and Whitton remained behind at the table.

"Are you alright?" Smith asked his wife.

"Fine," Whitton replied, and Smith knew she was anything but. "What's up?"

"I still don't know why you had to invite that woman," Whitton said. "She doesn't belong here."

"Please, Erica," Smith said. "Not now. Not tonight. Maybe if you got to know her a bit better, you'd change your opinion of her. She really isn't that bad."

"She's a whacko. A self-confessed one at that."

"Just give her a chance," Smith pleaded. "For my sake. Talk to her – if you still think she's certifiable when you're finished, I'll accept it. Now, let's get some food before this bunch of gluttonous police officers finish off the whole lot."

The food on the buffet table didn't last long. By the time Marge rang the bell for the second time that night, all that was left was a solitary scotch egg and a couple of cucumber sandwiches. Smith noticed that Bridge had been back to the table at least three times to refill his plate.

"Could we have a bit of hush, please?" Marge said. "It looks like you all enjoyed the food. Now, I'd like to say a few words about the birthday boy before he says a few, himself. I've known Jason Smith for a good few years. I've known him during good times and bad times, and I've seen him come through situations that would floor your average man. And he always emerges on the other side all the stronger for it. He's a good man – a good father and a good husband. And looking at you lot tonight, I'd say he's a good colleague too."

"Don't overdo it, Marge," Bridge chipped in. "He's got a big enough head as it is."

The whole room erupted. Smith had a huge grin on his face.

"I've said what I wanted to say," Marge said and looked at Smith. "Do you want to say a few words?"

"Not really, Marge."

"Chicken," Bridge said. "Speech. Speech. Speech."

Chalmers and Yang Chu joined in.

"Alright," Smith relented and approached the bar.

He looked at the crowd of people gathered in front of him. Most of them he'd worked with for years. These men and women had risked their lives for one another. Smith glanced over at his table and smiled. Whitton was sitting next to Jessica Blakemore. Jessica sat upright and still seemed very tense, but it was a start.

"Firstly," Smith began. "I'd like to say I'm glad I don't have to feed you lot on a daily basis. I don't think a detective sergeant's salary could run to it."

"You should know better than offering free food and booze to a bunch of Yorkshiremen," Chalmers shouted.

He'd obviously taken full advantage of the bar tab and was now very drunk.

"Thank you all for being here," Smith continued. "And thank you to Marge for putting on such a fine spread. My amazing wife, I know you and Baldwin helped organise this, and I really appreciate it. I know there's no more food, but the drinks are still on me."

He walked back to his table through a round of applause and pats on the back. Whitton and Jessica Blakemore were no longer there.

"Where's my amazing wife?" Smith asked Whitton's mum, Jane.

She was sitting with Laura on her lap. The youngest Smith was finding it hard to keep her eyes open.

"She went to the Ladies with that black-haired woman," Jane told him.

Smith was shocked. A short while ago Whitton had expressed nothing but contempt for the woman and now, she was accompanying her to the toilets.

Laura was now fast asleep on Jane's lap.

"She's lights out," Smith said. "I think we should take her home."

"You'll do no such thing," Jane said. "It's still early – you enjoy the rest of your party. Harold and I were thinking of heading off anyway. We'll take her with us."

"Are you sure?"

"Of course we are," Harold joined in. "You can pick her up in the morning. Enjoy the rest of your birthday."

Whitton and Jessica Blakemore emerged from the Ladies together. Both of them were grinning from ear to ear.

"What are you two smiling about?" Smith asked Whitton.

"Jessica was just filling me in on some of your less than finer moments," Whitton replied cryptically.

"What are you talking about?"

"You don't want to know," Jessica replied.

"Where are my mum and dad?" Whitton asked.

"Laura couldn't keep her eyes open, so they took her home. I don't know what we'd do without them."

"What's that?" Jessica pointed to something on the table.

It was a piece of paper. She leaned over and picked it up. It was the drawing Laura had been working on for most of the evening.

"This really is very good," Jessica said. "Did your daughter draw this?"

Smith took a look. It was a family portrait of sorts. In front of what was clearly Smith's red Ford Sierra stood a man and a woman and a child. Two dogs were lying on the ground at their feet.

"That looks nothing like me," Smith pointed to the man. "I don't have a red nose."

Whitton started to laugh. "You do sometimes, especially after a really rough night."

"It's very impressive anyway," Jessica added. "For someone so young I'd say she has a real talent."

"I didn't know you were into art," Smith said.

"I used to doodle in the hospital, remember. Painting is very therapeutic. It's incredible therapy. But seriously, you really should encourage your daughter."

"I'll give it some thought," Smith said as his mobile phone began to vibrate in his pocket.

He sighed and walked away from the table.

He didn't return to the table. He found DI Brownhill and placed his hand on her shoulder.

"Can I have a word, boss?"

"No work talk tonight," the DI was slurring her words.

"I'm afraid you need to hear this."

They moved to a quieter part of the pub.

"What is it?" the expression on Smith's face appeared to have sobered her up slightly.

"Bad news," Smith told her. "That was Doctor Howard from the hospital."

"Go on."

"It's about Haley Moore, the young woman who was brought in earlier. She didn't wake up. She lost too much blood and her organs simply shut down. She's dead, boss – our only witness is dead."

CHAPTER FORTY

Smith sat at the kitchen table with his head in his hands. He didn't feel in the least bit hungover – he was utterly dejected. The news of Haley Moore's death had hung over him like a dark cloud the whole night, and he'd hardly slept. He glanced at the untouched cup of coffee in front of him. They were back to square one. Four women had been killed in little more than a week and they had even less to go on now than they had a day earlier. Yesterday they not only had two promising suspects in custody, they had a potential witness. A woman had survived the attack, and she was the one person who could tell them who the killer was.

But now she was dead, and they had nothing.

"Penny for them," Whitton had come in the kitchen.

"What I'm thinking about right now isn't even worth a penny, Whitton," Smith turned to face his wife. "We're right back at the beginning, and I'm not sure I can summon up the energy to start all over again."

"Are you feeling sorry for yourself again? I told you, it doesn't suit you. We will crack this one."

"With what? Fairy dust? We have a killer who leaves nothing behind – we have no suspects, and as of last night, we have no witnesses."

"Maybe you should stop concentrating on what we don't have," Whitton suggested. "And put more energy into what we have got."

"Didn't you hear what I just said?"

"We know the victims knew their killer," Whitton ignored his self-pity. "We also have a good idea why the blood was taken. And there is a connection between all the dead women in that they were all students at the University."

"And we've explored all the avenues we could in that respect. Explored and exhausted."

"Then we'll explore them further," Whitton wasn't giving up. "We'll explore them until we do find something. Now could you please finish your coffee, have a shower and get ready for work. And when you come down those stairs, I expect you to behave more like the man I married and not some negative wimp."

* * *

"Sorry about earlier," Smith said to Whitton when they were roughly halfway to the station. "I really thought we were close to catching this killer when Haley Moore was left alive."

Whitton's parents had phoned and offered to look after Laura for the day, so there was no need to collect her and take her to day-care.

"That *negative wimp* thing was a bit harsh though," Smith added.

"Maybe," Whitton said. "But I can't stand watching you mope. It must be an age thing."

"If I wasn't driving, I'd slap you on the shoulder, Mrs Smith. At least we've got Smyth's stats presentation to look forward to later. That should be a real blast."

"If you say so."

"Thanks for making an effort with Jessica last night," Smith changed the subject.

"She's actually fun to talk to," Whitton admitted. "And I don't think she's mad in the head at all."

"Could I have that in writing?"

"Don't push it. And she's full of little anecdotes about you. I didn't realise you went to see her so many times in the nuthouse. She suggested we meet for coffee one afternoon. And I agreed."

"I think I'm going to regret pushing the two of you together."

They went inside the station and were greeted with a sombre silence. There wasn't the usual hum of voices around the front desk, and Smith didn't like it one little bit. Something was wrong.

"What's with the atmosphere in here today?" he asked Baldwin behind the desk. "It's like a morgue."

"I don't know," Baldwin replied. "But it doesn't look good. All I know is the DI was called into an emergency meeting with the Super and the Assistant Chief Constable first thing, and Brownhill didn't seem too pleased about it. I think it's to do with these recent murders."

Four murders and no progress had been made by the team working on the investigation, Smith thought.

That was clearly what was being discussed the emergency meeting, and Smith also knew full well from previous experience, heads were going to roll.

"Where are the rest of the team?" he asked Baldwin.

"Bridge hasn't turned up yet, but Yang Chu is up in the canteen. I can tell you, from the amount he had to drink last night Bridge is going to have a hangover from hell. God help him if he doesn't show his face before the DI get's out of the meeting."

Smith got himself and Whitton some coffee from the machine in the canteen and joined Yang Chu at his table.

"Have you heard from Bridge?" the young DC asked Smith. "I tried ringing him, but his phone goes straight to voicemail. He's going to be in deep shit if he's late today of all days. The Assistant Chief was already here when I arrived. Something's brewing and I don't like the look of it one little bit."

"Who exactly is the Assistant Chief these days?" Whitton asked. "I don't think I've even met him yet."

"Her," Yang Chu corrected her. "It's a woman. She only took over from old Lewis King a short while ago and she's still finding her feet."

"That usually translates to a shake-up," Smith said. "We'd better brace ourselves for a rough time ahead."

Bridge arrived shortly afterwards. He was unshaven and the shirt he was wearing was full of creases.

"What's going on around here?" he'd obviously also sensed the atmosphere in the station. "Everybody I bumped into downstairs looked like they were about to face a firing squad."

"You could be right there."

Smith informed him of the meeting that was taking place.

"What's the worst that can happen?" Bridge asked when Smith was finished.

"Didn't you hear a word I just said?" Smith said. "Smyth and Brownhill are in there right now with a new ACC. A woman who probably wants results early in her career as ACC. She's going to see straight through Smyth's bungling excuses and that's no doubt going to roll down to Brownhill. The DI is going to face the brunt of it, and where do you reckon that shit is going to end up?"

"All over our heads," Yang Chu answered the question.

"As if we weren't under enough pressure to crack this one before, now it's going to be unbearable. We need to catch this killer and we need to do it sharpish."

"Preferably before the press conference this evening," Brownhill had appeared in the doorway.

"How did the meeting go, boss?" Smith asked her. "What's the new ACC like? Full of energy and out to change the world?"

Brownhill got some coffee and sat down. "She wasn't at all like I expected. I'd braced myself for an ear bashing, and with Smyth there too I expected the worst, but it all went rather pleasantly. ACC Greene was very accommodating. She asked where we stood in the investigation, and when I outlined the case, she merely asked what she could do to help."

"You're kidding?" Smith said.

"No. She asked what assistance she could offer to help further the investigation. Superintendent Smyth barely said a word throughout the whole meeting."

"Probably for the best," Smith said. "And what did you say?"

"I told her I would request assistance should it become necessary. And that my team were working round the clock, and not leaving anything unchecked."

"But we've got nothing, boss," Smith reminded her. "Sod all. Our only witness is dead. Where do you suggest we go from here?"

"Back to the beginning. Small conference room in five minutes."

CHAPTER FORTY ONE

The artist moved so close to the canvas that the tip of her nose almost touched the final layer of *paint*. The blood was still wet, and this was when the intoxicating metallic tang was most exquisite. The artist breathed in deeply, held the air in her lungs for as long as possible then exhaled onto the scene in front of her.

This one was different to the rest – this was a landscape with its own story. The *paint* used had been more costly that the *paint* on the others.

There was one more painting to complete, and then the artist would be finished. She could finally return home, back to where she really belonged. There would be no denying her that anymore.

But before then she had one more obstacle to overcome, and it would be the hardest thing she'd ever had to do.

CHAPTER FORTY TWO

The large white board on the wall in the small conference room looked brand new.

"Where did that come from?" Smith asked Brownhill.

"It was time for a clean slate," the DI told him. "I was tired of looking at faded snippets from past cases. Do you want to do the honours?"

"With pleasure." Smith approached the board and picked up a black marker. "From the beginning. Kirsty King." He started to write on the board. "Twenty-year-old law second-year law student. One of her housemates called us because of a noxious smell coming from Kirsty's room. She'd already been dead four or five days when her body was discovered."

Smith stopped there, then wrote in block capitals, 'Drained of blood.'

"TOD was confirmed at sometime around the previous weekend. Kirsty was alone in the house the whole weekend. There were only two keys for her room – one of them was found locked inside the room, and the other was on a key holder in the hallway."

He wrote on the board once more. 'Traces of Flunitrazepam found in her system.'

Smith repeated the procedure for Taylor Fox, Rene Downs and Haley Moore. He wrote all relevant information on the board and connected all similarities with black lines. When he was finished, the board resembled a join-the-dots picture.

"It's not pretty, but there you have it. What we have are four young women. All of them were students at the University – all of them were drugged first and all of them had their blood removed. As far as we know they weren't friends. They barely knew one another. We still do not have a scene of crime for the murder of Taylor Fox, but at the other three there was no sign of any kind of struggle. That suggests they knew who was about to kill them. Have I missed anything?"

"The Flunitrazepam," Bridge said. "Where did the killer get it? As far as I'm aware, it's not something you can get over the counter at a Chemist."

"Good," Smith said. "We'll look into it. Anything else?"

"That acronym," Yang Chu said. "The one that was written next to an appointment time on Taylor Fox's laptop. PS. We still haven't figured out what it stands for."

"It could stand for anything, Yang Chu," Smith said. "And we don't have time to waste on word puzzles."

Grant Webber entered the room. He had an expression on his face that Smith had seen many times before. It was an expression that meant he'd found something.

"You've got something for us, haven't you?" Smith said.

"I believe I have," the head of forensics replied. "It might not mean much, but the bloody footprint we found on the carpet in Haley Moore's bedroom has been identified."

"What do you mean identified?" Smith asked.

"Don't get too excited," Webber said. "We haven't found who it belongs to, but we do have a size and a make. Doc Martens. Shoes, size five. The tread on a pair of Docs are unmistakable."

Smith sighed. "Thanks, Webber, but the majority of the student population of York probably own a pair of Doc Martens."

Then something occurred to him. He remembered something Jessica Blakemore had said. Something he considered at the time, but then put to the back of his head.

"Size five? That's pretty small feet. I assume you checked to see it didn't match any of Miss Moore's housemate's shoes?"

"Please do not insult my intelligence."

"Sorry, Webber," Smith said. "My mouth was ahead of my brain there. Size five shoes. If our killer was wearing size five shoes, it's pretty safe to assume we're looking at a woman here."

"We do not assume anything," Brownhill said. "There are plenty of men out there with small feet, and vice versa. I happen to wear a size ten."

"But you're an exceptional woman, boss. It all makes sense."

"What makes sense?"

"Think about it. We've established these four women all knew the person who killed them. If you were a woman, who would you not think twice about inviting into your house? Who would you feel least threatened by?"

"Another woman," Whitton said.

Nobody spoke for a few seconds. Brownhill was the first to break the silence.

"You could very well be onto something."

"Well, at least we can exclude fifty percent of the population now," Bridge said, and the DI glared at him.

"It still doesn't help us," Bridge carried on. "We had two suspects – both men, and both were in custody when the latest murder was carried out. How exactly does knowing the sex of this maniac help us?"

"You're right," Smith said. "You're right about excluding fifty percent of the population. At least we can stop looking in the wrong places."

"Do you even have any suspects in mind?" Bridge was far from finished.

"What about Dr Dessai?" Whitton asked and immediately put her hand over her mouth.

Smith let out a long sigh. "You're right. We need to bring her in and interview her."

He went on to tell the other people in the room about the former head of pathology's past indiscretions.

"And that's why she requested a transfer to another department," Smith said in closing.

"And you didn't think this relevant to the investigation?" Brownhill looked furious.

"We've spoken to her," Smith said. "In private. I gave Kenny Bean my word and I thought discretion would be the best policy in the interests of Dr Dessai's future career prospects."

"I cannot believe I'm hearing this. You do realise how this is going to look if it turns out that this woman *is* involved in these murders and you withheld information highly relevant to the investigation?"

"It was pointed out to me, boss," Smith said and glanced at his wife. "Like I said, we'll bring her in and speak to her. I get a feeling we're barking up the wrong tree with Dr Dessai though."

"I am not basing the direction of a murder investigation on another one of your feelings."

"With respect, Ma'am," Whitton joined in. "Surely all we have to ascertain is her whereabouts on the days in question and her shoe size. We can rule her out immediately if she has alibis for the days the murders were carried out. It's not necessary to bring up mistakes she's made in the past."

"Inform her that her presence is required here as soon as possible. We'll see what she has to say, and we'll take it from there. Smith, as you wish to be discreet, you and Whitton can carry out the interview. Bridge, you and Yang Chu can look into the Flunitrazepam. Find out about possible sources of the drug. Does anybody have any questions?"

"This new Assistant Chief Constable, Ma'am," Bridge said. "I heard a rumour she's a bit of a looker. What's she like?"

"Totally out of your league, DS Bridge," Brownhill informed him. "Now, can we please get down to business."

CHAPTER FORTY THREE

When Smith and Whitton walked down the corridor in the hospital towards Dr Kenny Bean's office, Smith suddenly realised how much time he'd actually spent within the walls of the hospital over the past year or so. He'd spent weeks in a hospital bed after almost having his heart removed – two weeks in intensive care followed by another few months of recovery, then after a near-fatal skydiving accident he'd been resident for another few weeks. The hospital was becoming a home from home. Whitton had even joked that he'd be receiving Christmas cards from the staff soon.

The thought made him feel anxious.

He'd just celebrated his thirty-sixth birthday and he'd already lost count of how many times he'd come close to death.

It couldn't go on.

Maybe it is time to do something else, he thought, for the sake of Whitton and Laura, maybe it was time for a change of career.

"Detectives," a familiar voice broke Smith's reverie.

It was Kenny Bean.

The Head of Pathology had just come out of his office.

"If this is about your birthday bash," he said to Smith. "I couldn't get away. You know what it's like. Happy Birthday for yesterday by the way."

"It's not about my birthday," Smith told him. "We're looking for Dr Dessai."

"I seem to recall her transferring to another department."

"I know, but we can't find her in the endoscopic department. She was supposed to be at work, but nobody has seen her today."

"Then I assume she's not at work today," Dr Bean said with a touch of irony in his voice.

"And you haven't seen her?" Whitton asked.

"We very rarely cross paths these days – her department is on the other side of the hospital."

Smith realised this wasn't strictly true – twice now they'd seen Dr Dessai on the pathology wing.

"Do you know where she lives?" he asked.

"Of course, I know where she lives. What exactly is this all about?"

"We need to ask her a few more questions," Whitton said.

"Could we have that address, please?" Smith added.

Smith stopped his car outside the address Kenny Bean had given them for Dr Dessai. Dr Bean had been reluctant at first, but when Smith had explained it was probably something over nothing, he'd relented and given it to them.

"Doctors must do alright for themselves," Whitton commented as they got out the car and stood outside the house. It was situated in a relatively new estate just one row up from the river. All the houses were free-standing and all of them had fairly large gardens in front.

"I bet this cost a few bob," Whitton added.

Smith knocked on the door and they waited. He knocked again then noticed there was a doorbell partially hidden by a layer of dirt on the wall next to the door. He pressed it and heard the musical tone of the bell inside the house.

"You couldn't fail to hear that," he said to Whitton.

They waited a few more seconds.

"It looks like there's nobody home," Whitton said. "Where do you think she is?"

"She's not at work where she's supposed to be," Smith said. "And she's clearly not at home, so your guess is as good as mine."

He stepped back a few paces and looked at the house. The curtains downstairs were open but upstairs they were closed on the largest of the three windows. Smith was sure he saw something move upstairs. "Did you see that?" he said to Whitton. "There's a curtain twitcher upstairs."

Whitton looked up but the curtains were now still. "I think you need your eyes checked."

"I know what I saw," Smith said and stepped forward to ring the doorbell once more.

The door still did not open. Smith placed his hand on the doorknob. "What are you doing?" Whitton said.

"There is definitely somebody inside that house,"

Smith turned the doorknob and the door opened.

"Dr Dessai," he shouted from inside. "Police, we need to talk to you."

He stepped inside the house and, immediately a familiar smell hit the inside of his nose. It was vaguely chemical, but there was something else about it that made Smith's stomach heat up and his heart started to beat faster.

"Dr Dessai," he called out again. "It's DS Smith. We need to talk to you."

She appeared at the top of the stairs. She was dressed in a pair of jeans and a white smock. The smock was covered in paint.

"What do you want?" she shouted down.

"Please come down," Smith told her, "We need you to come with us."

"What for?"

Smith was running out of patience. He didn't have time for this. He made his way up the stairs. Whitton followed behind him. Dr Dessai disappeared inside a room and Smith heard the click of a lock on the other side of a door.

"Open that door," he demanded. "We just need to ask you some questions and you're not doing yourself any favours."

"What's this all about?" a muffled voice was heard from behind the locked door.

"Open up," Smith had had enough. "Or I'll open the door myself. It's your choice."

He heard a noise inside the room. It sounded like glass being thrown into a bin.

"Stand back, Whitton," he said. "I'm going to open the door."

He looked at the door handle, leaned back and raised his foot into the air. He was glad he was wearing the shoes with the tough soles. He aimed his foot next to the door handle and kicked the door as hard as he could.

"Fuck." A searing pain shot up his leg and his foot started to throb. The door splintered next to the handle and shot open.

Smith limped inside. He could see straight away that this was where Dr Dessai painted. Four easels were set up in front of the window. Two of them were covered in white sheets but the images on the other two were very familiar. They were both landscapes and both of them were very similar in their reddish-brown colours. More paintings stood on the floor against the wall. Dr Dessai was cowering in the corner. She resembled a hare caught in the headlights of an oncoming car. She looked absolutely terrified.

"What the hell is going on?" Smith asked her. "Why didn't you answer the door? And why did you lock yourself in here?"

The doctor remained silent.

"Why aren't you at work today?" Whitton asked her.

Dr Dessai looked at her. "I wanted to paint."

"That doesn't explain why you hid away from us," Smith said and removed the sheet from one of the covered paintings.

It was also a landscape - it had clearly been painted very recently, and it bore a striking resemblance to the small landscape that was pushed through his letterbox the day before. The paint was still wet in places. Smith dabbed a finger against the wet paint and raised it to his nose. There was definitely something metallic about the smell.

"Is this blood?"

"Of course not," Dr Dessai rose to her feet. "Of course it's not blood. It's oil paint."

Smith turned to his wife. "Whitton get Webber and his team here right now. I want all of these paintings analysed."

Whitton took out her phone and left the room.

"Did you deliver a painting to my house yesterday?" Smith asked Dr Dessai. "A small landscape very similar to the ones in here?"

"Of course not. Why would I do that?"

"All it had on the envelope it was in was my name and 'Happy Birthday.'"

"Firstly," Dr Dessai said. "I wasn't aware it was your birthday, and secondly, I have no idea where you live."

Smith thought this over. If that was the case, who did in fact send him the painting? He glanced around the room. The painting of the limestone formations of the Pinnacles Desert was still clear in his head. He was no expert on art, but quite a few of the paintings in Dr Dessai's studio were very similar.

Too similar.

"Dr Rani Dessai," Smith said. "I'm arresting you for the murders of Kirsty King, Taylor Fox, Rene Downs and Haley Moore."

He reeled off her rights and placed his arm on her shoulder.
"I'm going to arrange for a car to come and pick you up. Why did you make me kick the door in? I'm going to be walking with a limp for weeks."

CHAPTER FORTY FOUR

"Flunitrazepam," Bridge said.

He and DC Yang Chu sat in DI Brownhill's office.

"Flunitrazepam is a sedative-hypnotic," Bridge continued to read from a sheet of paper. "Also known as Rohypnol. It is a central nervous system depressant – class Benzodiazepines, used generally to treat anxiety, insomnia and other sleep disorders. Because of its emergence as a date-rape drug, it was reclassified, and stricter records had to be kept on its distribution. It's actually banned in certain states in America."

"That's all well and good," Brownhill said. "But how does that help us find out who can get their hands on the stuff?"

"I'm getting to that, Ma'am," Bridge said. "The effects of the drug are quick, especially when mixed with alcohol, and the affected person will have no idea what is happening around them. Mercifully, these women won't have felt a thing. The prescription of this drug is very carefully monitored – records have to be kept, and it is definitely not something you can buy over the counter at Boots."

"So, have you checked the recent records?"

"I don't think that will help, Ma'am," Yang Chu said.

"What do you mean? Are you telling me the result of a whole morning's work is half a piece of paper?"

"We've been through the records," Bridge explained. "But we might have a problem there."

"I don't like the sound of that," the DI said.

"Rohypnol is not only used in the medical world – it's making a name for itself as a recreational drug, and it is quite addictive. Users take it with alcohol, marijuana, LSD. And that leads us to our problem."

"It's available on the black market?" Brownhill knew what was coming next.

"Precisely, Ma'am," Yang Chu said. "And you know what that means. Anybody with ready cash can get hold of it if they know where to look."

"And the suppliers are hardly likely to tell us who they've sold the stuff to," Bridge added.

"So, where does that leave us?" Brownhill asked.

"With a morning wasted," Bridge replied.

Brownhill's mobile phone started to ring. She picked it up.

"Smith, what did you get from Dr Dessai?"

Bridge and Yang Chu watched as the DI listened intently to what Smith was saying on the other end of the line. Her face didn't give anything away.

"Get back here straight away," she spoke into the phone and ended the call.

She rubbed her eyes and turned to stare out of the window.

"Has Smith found something?" Yang Chu asked.

"Dr Dessai has been arrested," Brownhill said. "She's on her way here now. I have something urgent to attend to. Bridge, I want you and Yang Chu to carry out the interview with Dr Dessai."

"I thought Smith was going to interview her," Bridge looked confused.

"Not anymore," Brownhill's eyes seemed to become darker. "Not anymore."

* * *

Chalmers was in his office poring through some paperwork when Brownhill walked in. The DCI looked extremely bored.

"Sir," Brownhill said. "Can I have a word?"

"Of course," Chalmers looked up from the papers. "Anything to distract me from this crime stat bollocks. Take a seat. From the look on your face, I take it this isn't just a social call."

"We've got a serious problem, sir," Brownhill sat down and came straight to the point.

"Go on."

"It's about Smith."

Chalmers sighed. "I knew it couldn't last."

"Sir?"

"Smith has kept his nose clean for far too long – something had to give. What's he done now?"

"This is serious," Brownhill said. "I came to you because, quite frankly, I don't know what to do."

Chalmers got up from his desk and closed the door of his office.

"Spit it out, Bryony," he said when he'd sat back down.

"Smith and Whitton went to see the former head of pathology," Brownhill said. "Dr Dessai. She didn't turn up for work this morning, and when they went to her house, it appeared there was nobody home. She was hiding upstairs. Unfortunately for her, she'd forgotten to lock the door, and Smith found her upstairs in her art studio. She locked herself in. The way she reacted when they came in the house aroused suspicion, and that, together with the nature of the paintings in her studio gave Smith reasonable grounds to arrest her."

"Am I missing something here?" Chalmers asked. "I don't see any problems."

"There's more, sir. Smith received a painting in the post yesterday – a landscape that was very similar to the ones found in Dr Dessai's studio. Whitton has gone to fetch it so Grant can go over it and compare it to the ones painted by Dr Dessai."

"So, Smith neglected to mention he'd received a painting in the post? Where are you going with this?"

"Earlier in the week, Smith spoke to Kenny Bean about Dr Dessai," Brownhill took a deep breath. "It was an informal chat at the pub, but Dr Bean opened up about his past relationship with Dr Dessai. He told Smith in confidence about why Dr Dessai no longer worked in Pathology and why she was transferred to another department. He caught her red-handed taking blood from the lab. She later confessed that she'd been using this blood to experiment with in her art. Smith kept his promise to Kenny Bean and it only came out later in one of the case meetings. Even though Smith had information that was definitely relevant to the investigation, Dr Dessai was never formally interviewed. As soon as I found out about it, I instructed Smith to speak to Dr Dessai – he wanted to be discreet to safeguard her future career prospects, and as such I don't believe he really dug as deep as he ought to."

"Let me get this straight," Chalmers scratched his head. "Because Smith kept the word of a friend, and because he didn't want to tarnish the reputation of a doctor you think he acted unprofessionally? The woman's on her way here isn't she? She's been arrested. If she's innocent, we'll find out, and if she's not that's the end of it."

"No, it's not," Brownhill raised her voice. "If Smith had shared the info he had on Dr Dessai earlier, Haley Moore, the young woman who was killed yesterday might still be alive."

CHAPTER FORTY FIVE

Chalmers intercepted Smith before he'd even made it through the doors of the station.

"My other office, now," the DCI put his hand on Smith's shoulder and directed him round the back of the station where it was more sheltered from the biting wind.

It was here where Smith and Chalmers took their smoke breaks when the weather was bad. Chalmers lit up a cigarette and handed the packet to Smith.

Smith lit one and handed the pack back. "You've heard then?"

"You've pulled some stunts in your time," Chalmers rubbed his hands together. "But this time you've really outdone yourself. What the hell were you thinking?"

"I didn't think anything. I've known Dr Dessai for a long time, and even though she's been arrested, something in me doesn't think she killed those women."

"For your sake, you'd better pray your gut is right."

"How's the DI taking it? I suppose she wants my head on a plate."

"No," Chalmers exhaled a cloud of smoke. "Brownhill is on your side. She could have taken this right to the top, but she came to me first. She's got your back, for what it's worth. How many other people know about this?"

"The whole team," Smith admitted. "And now you. Oh, and Kenny Bean of course."

"That's a lot of people's careers we're talking about, Smith. Fuck it, why couldn't you have just brought the woman in straight away? If the press gets wind that you neglected to act on information vital to the investigation and a young woman was killed because of it, the whole

York Police Force is going to be in the shit. I thought that having a child might make you grow up a bit."

Smith threw his cigarette on the ground and stood on it. "I have grown up, boss. I've grown up a lot, and I've been doing a hell of a lot of thinking. Nobody else has to suffer because I happened to promise not to break the confidence of a friend, because, in essence that's all I did. If the press want to see it in another way, that's their problem."

"Don't be so bloody naive, lad," Chalmers glared at him. "The press couldn't give a bollocks about your misplaced loyalty – all they care about is a meaty story, and this is as meaty as it gets. I can just see the headline now. 'Student dies due to police negligence'."

"Then I'll go down alone," Smith held the DCI's stare. "I'll come clean about withholding the information and make it very clear that nobody else in the team knew about it. I'll bring it up at the press conference later. I've been seriously considering a change of career anyway."

"You will do no such thing," Chalmers took out another cigarette. "This is how we're going to play it. Bridge and Yang Chu will be conducting the interview with Dr Dessai. If your famous gut is right and it turns out she had nothing to do with these murders, that will be the end of it. Nobody has to mention it again. But I'll tell you one thing, and this is a direct order. You keep your mouth shut at that press conference."

* * *

"Interview with Dr Rani Dessai commenced 13:45," Bridge began. "Present DS Bridge, DC Yang Chu and Mr Howe, Dr Dessai's legal representation. Dr Dessai, are you aware of why you were arrested?"

"I've advised my client to answer all of your questions truthfully," the lawyer answered for her.

That'll be a first, Bridge thought.

"I don't even know why I hid from them," Dr Dessai said.

"You're referring to your unusual behaviour when DS Smith and DC Whitton called at your house earlier today?" Bridge said. "For the record."

Dr Dessai nodded her head.

"For the tape, Dr Dessai is nodding her head. Why exactly did you pretend you weren't at home?"

"I panicked. I was scared."

"Scared of what?" Yang Chu asked her.

"Scared that all of it might come out and I might lose my job."

"You work at the hospital in the endoscopy department?" Bridge said. "Is that correct?"

"Yes."

"Forgive me, but what exactly is endoscopy?"

"It's a non-surgical medical procedure whereby a tube is inserted inside the body to get a better picture of what's wrong."

"But you used to be head of department in pathology," Bridge said. "Is that right?"

"I transferred last year."

"Could you tell us why you left a post as head of department to move to another part of the hospital? Surely that was somewhat of a demotion."

Dr Dessai glanced at her lawyer for advice.

"Just answer the question," was the advice Mr Howe gave.

"I made a terrible mistake," Dr Dessai said. "I like to paint in my spare time, and I was experimenting with new materials."

She stopped for a few seconds and Bridge decided to let her finish.

She took a deep breath. "I was caught taking blood from the lab."

"You stole blood from the pathology lab?" Bridge said.

"It was only a few vials, and my experimental stage didn't come to anything, but the damage was done. It would have cost me my career if it came out, but I was offered a solution. If I transferred to another department, I was assured that would be the end of it. This isn't going to be made public is it?"

"I cannot answer that," Bridge said. "Let's concentrate on what happened earlier this morning."

"Could I please have some water?" Dr Dessai asked.

Yang Chu got up and left the room. He returned a few minutes later with two bottles of water.

"When DS Smith found you in your studio earlier," Bridge carried on. "You were crouched on the floor. Can you explain why that was?"

"I told you," Dr Dessai said. "I was scared. I really felt like my whole life was over. I didn't kill those women."

"What size shoe do you wear, Dr Dessai?" Yang Chu asked.

"Is that really relevant?" Mr Howe asked.

"Extremely," Bridge replied. "Please answer the question, Dr Dessai."

"Size four, or sometimes a size five when I'm wearing thick socks."

"In the winter for example?"

"Yes."

"And can you remember what shoes you were wearing yesterday?"

"Probably my black work shoes – it was icy outside, and they have good soles."

Bridge took out a sheet of paper. On it were the names of the four women who were murdered and the dates of those murders.

"Dr Dessai, I need you to think hard and try and remember where you were on the following days. Saturday 27 January."

"How am I supposed to remember that?" she directed the question at her lawyer. "That's ten days ago."

"Please try and think," Mr Howe advised her.

"Let me help you out," Bridge said.

They had contacted human resources at the hospital and were given a list of Dr Dessai's shifts for the past two weeks.

"You weren't at work on the twenty-seventh," he told her. "Can you remember what you did on that day? Specifically, in the afternoon?"

"I can't remember."

"What about last Wednesday the thirty-first?"

"I was at work last Wednesday," Dr Dessai replied with a smile on her face.

"Only until noon," Bridge reminded her. "What is it doctors call it? Half-day Wednesday? Can you remember what you did in the afternoon?"

"I think I did some shopping," she replied. "I normally do my shopping at the end of the month."

"OK," Bridge said. "We'll need a bit more than that. Till and credit card receipts."

Bridge knew that Dr Dessai hadn't been at work on the days the final two women were killed, and, as she failed to provide any kind of alibis for these two days, he also knew they were justified in holding her for at least another forty-eight hours to give forensics time to analyse everything they'd found at her house. Her lawyer didn't even try and protest.

"Interview with Dr Rani Dessai finished 14:15," Bridge said and turned off the recording device.

CHAPTER FORTY SIX

Smith had been sitting the canteen just staring out of the window for almost two hours when Bridge and Yang Chu came in. Bridge was beaming from ear to ear.

"It looks like it's all over," he said and patted Smith on the back. "You were the one who arrested her, so they'll probably pin a medal on you. They might even promote you to DI."

"What is he on about?" Smith asked Yang Chu.

"Dr Dessai has all but confessed," Bridge got in before Yang Chu had a chance to reply.

"She didn't confess," the young DC said. "There were just a few things that she couldn't explain."

"A few things?" Bridge exclaimed. "She's our bloodthirsty artist. Even without a confession we've got more than enough for a conviction. Any judge and jury would put her away. She has a history of painting in blood, a shoeprint matching the size she wears was found at the last crime scene, and she doesn't have an alibi for any of the dates the murders were carried out. Add all that to the fact she's a doctor and can probably get hold of enough Rohypnol to fell a horse and I'd say a good few celebratory drinks are in order after the press conference this evening."

Smith rose to his feet and stood facing Bridge. From the expression on his face, and his aggressive body language Yang Chu was afraid he was going to punch Bridge in the face. Bridge must have sensed something too because he backed off slightly.

"Circumstantial," Smith said.

The smell of alcohol on his breath made Bridge step back even further.

"Everything you just said is all fucking circumstantial," Smith said. "Every last bit of it. When are you going to wake up and start acting like a detective sergeant?"

He barged past Bridge before he had a chance to digest what Smith had just said.

"What's his problem?" Bridge said. "You'd think he'd be over the moon about catching the murderer."

"You never can tell what's going on in Smith's head," Yang Chu mused. "You ought to know that by now."

"He's losing the plot. That's all I can say."

"Who's losing the plot?" It was Chalmers.

The DCI had come in without them realising.

"Smith, sir," Bridge told him. "It looks like this Dr Dessai is odds on favourite for the recent murders and Smith acted like it was the worst news in the world."

"Shit," Chalmers said. "Where is Smith now?"

"I have no idea, sir," Bridge said. "As far away from me as possible if he knows what's good for him. He's been drinking, too. I could smell it on his breath."

* * *

Smith hadn't been drinking. Not in the way Bridge had assumed anyway. He kept a bottle of Jack Daniel's tucked away in a drawer in his office and he'd taken a swig after speaking to Chalmers. He was still under the legal limit to drive. He sat in his car and banged his hands against the steering wheel until they began to throb. He didn't know what to do. If it transpired that Dr Rani Dessai was in fact the person who had killed four women recently, Smith knew he could kiss his job goodbye. But that wasn't the worst part. He could live with losing his job. If he'd acted on the information Kenny Bean had given him and Dr Dessai had been apprehended earlier, Haley Moore would still be alive. A woman in the prime of her life was dead because Smith was stupid enough to keep a secret for a friend.

It was a nightmare. He took out his phone and dialled Whitton's number. She answered immediately.

"Where are you?" he asked.

"I'm at home. Brownhill told me to take a couple of hours off before the crime stats thing. Where are you?"

"Sitting in my car debating whether to go out and get rat-arsed or not."

"What's happened?"

Smith filled her in on the events following his arrest of Dr Dessai.

"What if it was her, Whitton?" he said when he'd finished. "What if she did kill all those women? I should have arrested her earlier. Haley Moore is dead because I didn't. She's dead because of a stupid promise I made to Kenny Bean."

"Calm down," Whitton said. "We don't know yet that Dr Dessai is our killer. You're right – everything we have is circumstantial, so wait and see what else turns up. Wait and see what Webber comes up with in forensics before you start jumping to conclusions and go off and do something stupid."

"Maybe it's fate."

"What?"

"You know I've been talking about doing something else? Maybe this is a way of making sure I do. This is a mistake I won't be able to come back from. It's fate."

"That's the biggest load of crap I've heard in years," Whitton said and added in a softer voice. "Come home. Come home and have something to eat before the crime stats/press conference later."

"I just need to check something first," Smith told her. "I'll be home when I'm finished."

He rang off without offering any further explanation.

CHAPTER FORTY SEVEN

Jessica Blakemore didn't look too happy to see Smith standing on the path outside her house when she opened the door. She didn't even try and disguise her disapproval.

"What do you want?"

"It's lovely to see you too," Smith said. "I need some advice."

"Of course you do. Come in but make it quick. I was about to go out."

Smith sat on an armchair in the living room and stretched out his arms.

"Don't make yourself too comfortable," Jessica told him. "I'm going out remember."

"Where are you going?"

"That's none of your business. What do you want?"

A rather large ginger Tom ambled in the room. It looked Smith up and down with nonchalant eyes and curled up on the two-seater settee opposite him. Jessica sat down next to it.

"That's weird," she said. "Pete doesn't normally like strangers. You must be harmless."

"Animals seem to like me," Smith said. "I think I've done something really stupid."

"And here was me thinking you were going to entertain me with something new. What is it you think you've done?"

"I withheld information in an investigation," Smith told her. "And because of that a young woman died."

Jessica's face softened slightly. "What did you do?"

"I had something I should have shared with the team, but I kept it to myself because I gave my word to a friend."

"A moral dilemma of the worst kind. Go on."

"The detective in me knew this was extremely relevant to the ongoing investigation."

"But the human being in you couldn't betray the confidence of a friend?" Jessica finished his sentence. "What is it you want me to tell you? I'm not a priest, Jason – this is not a confessional. What do you want?"

"I don't think it's about what I want. I think it's about what's been decided for me. Fate."

"I don't believe in fate," Jessica said. "I learned a long time ago there is no such thing as fate. We make our own fate. We learn from our past and we determine our own future. Have you found religion all of a sudden?"

"No. I don't know. What I'm trying to say is maybe what is happening here is merely my subconscious telling me what my conscious already knows is the right thing to do."

"Psycho babble if ever I've heard it. And it doesn't wash with an ex-shrink. Do you know what I think?"

"I wouldn't be here if I did."

"I think you're really just totally exhausted, and the reason for that is your own doing."

"What do you mean by that?" Smith asked.

"Don't come here again, Jason. I'm getting tired of offering you the same advice over and over and you never listening. I'll say it one more time and then that's it. No more. You are one man. You take on the responsibilities of the world even though nobody expects you to. Learn to understand that you don't need to do it. Step back and accept help when it's offered to you. Because if you don't, you're going to lose everything you care about."

The room was silent for a while. Jessica Blakemore watched Smith's face as he seemed to digest everything she'd just told him. "Thanks, Jessica," he said and stood up. "I think you're right. I'm making this into more than it is. You've been a great help. I won't bother you again. Can I ask you just one more question?"

"If you insist."

"Can we still go out for the odd drink now and then?"

"Get out," Jessica said, although it was clear she was trying hard to suppress the smile that was trying to break through.

* * *

Whitton was feeding Laura at the kitchen table when Smith got home. She turned to look at her husband standing in the doorway. "Are you alright?"

Smith could feel that something was happening inside him. He didn't know exactly what chemical reactions were occurring deep inside his body, but he knew that something was about to give. His jaw began to quiver, a tingling spread from his mouth up past his nose and stopped at his left eye. Then the tears came. First, they came in tiny droplets but then he couldn't stop the alarming flow that came from his eyes. He could taste the salty tears on his lips when they reached his mouth. Whitton didn't speak. She walked over and wrapped her arms around Smith. His arms found their way around her back and they just held each other. Smith didn't want to let go.

It was Whitton who broke off the embrace. Laura was oblivious to the scene that had just played out mere metres away. She was more interested in polishing off what was left of her mashed potatoes and carrots.

Smith managed to stem the tears enough to speak. "Sorry, I don't have a clue what just happened."

Whitton smiled.

"Are you alright?" she asked him again.

Smith wiped his eyes. "I am. I am now."

"There's some of my mum's casserole in the microwave. It just needs warming up. I'm going to have a shower."

Smith watched her as she left the room. He realised his mouth was wide open. His little outburst had surprised him, but what surprised him more was his wife's reaction to it. It was as though it didn't surprise her in the least. It was almost as if she'd been expecting it.

CHAPTER FORTY EIGHT

The car park at the station was almost full when Smith and Whitton arrived just before 5pm. The crime stats presentation cum press conference wasn't due to start for at least another hour so Smith knew most of the cars belonged to York Police employees. The representatives of the press wouldn't have arrived yet. No sooner had they stepped inside the station, Smith and Whitton were approached by Neil Walker. The press liaison officer was dressed smartly as usual. He was wearing an expensive-looking dark blue suit with a white shirt and rather bright pink tie.

"Can I have a word?" he asked Smith.

"I'm here merely as an observer," Smith told him. "I've had my orders."

"Change of plan. You've done this kind of thing before. Besides, the crime stats thing will be the main event – you'll just be the support act."

"What a horrible thought."

"DI Brownhill is waiting in her office," Walker said.

"You head up to the canteen," Smith told Whitton. "I'll be up there when we're finished."

Neil Walker led Smith down the corridor, and they stopped outside DI Brownhill's office. The door was open, so they went straight in. The DI was sitting behind her desk.

"Take a seat. This won't take long."

Smith and Walker sat opposite her.

"I just wanted to give you a heads up," Brownhill spoke directly to Smith. "Even though the press were invited to attend this evening, this is mostly pertaining to the crime statistics. Naturally we are anticipating some questions regarding the ongoing investigation – it can't be helped, but we cannot afford to give them too much. Neil."

"Thank you, Bryony," the press liaison officer said. "These days news travels fast, what with social media and such, so the fact that we have a suspect in custody will no doubt already be common knowledge. We will be asked about it, and we can confirm it, but until more evidence comes to light, that's about all we can do."

"Same as always then," Smith said without an ounce of sarcasm in his tone.

"Same as always," Walker agreed.

"Does he know about the other stuff?" Smith asked Brownhill.

"What other stuff?" the press liaison officer obviously didn't know about it.

"That's not important," Brownhill said and quickly changed the subject. "Superintendent Smyth's crime statistics presentation will probably bore the pants out of the press, so hopefully they'll all be in a hurry to get away as quickly as possible, but Neil has decided we keep to bare facts when pressed about the current investigation. Four women have been killed. We have a suspect and forensics are still busy analysing potential evidence."

"So, we don't mention the blood then?" Smith said.

"It might be brought up," Walker admitted. "And if it is, we don't deny it, but we do not speculate on why blood was taken. I think that about covers it."

"Thank you, Neil," Brownhill said. "Smith could I have a word in private?"

"Close the door," the DI said to Smith when the press liaison officer had left.

Smith did as he was asked and sat back down. "What's going on?"

"Are you alright?" Brownhill said.

"I'm fine," Smith replied. "You're the second person to ask me that in the space of just over an hour. "I feel loved."

"I'm concerned about you," Brownhill ignored his last remark. "I'm concerned that you feel you have to take full responsibility for withholding what Dr Bean told you in confidence."

"I'm coming to terms with it, boss."

"You don't have to," Brownhill continued. "I've thought hard about it, and I see no reason why it should ever be brought up."

"I appreciate your concern, but you know as well as I do how these things have a habit of coming out when you least expect them to. I will not drag any of the team down with me. I will take full responsibility. It was my balls-up."

"I'm afraid it's too late for that," Brownhill said. "If we uncover damning evidence to back up what we already have on Dr Dessai it's inevitable that it will come to light that you spoke to her regarding her past transgressions before Haley Moore was killed."

"I know that," Smith said. "But I said I'll accept full responsibility for it."

"And I told you it's too late for that. I've spoken to DCI Chalmers, and we've agreed on a plan of action should that situation arise. The DCI and I were both well aware of your conversation with Dr Dessai prior to the murder of Haley Moore."

"But you weren't, boss."

"Yes, we were," Brownhill insisted. "And I'm afraid it's not open for debate. I will not let one of my finest detectives have to run the kind of gauntlet that this will attract on his own."

Smith was speechless. He and Brownhill had slowly reached some kind of understanding over the years, but never in a million years had he expected the DI to actually put her neck on the line to back him up."

"I can't let you do that, boss."

"I'll say it one last time," Brownhill said and rose from her chair to indicate the conversation was over. "It's too late for that."

Smith also stood up. He had an overwhelming urge to lean over and hug his DI, but he shrugged it off. He turned around and left the office without saying anything further.

CHAPTER FORTY NINE

"Ladies and Gentlemen," Superintendent Jeremy Smyth began another of his annual cringe-worthy crime statistics presentations.

A collective groan could be heard from the people sitting before him in the large conference room. It wasn't only the employees of York Police who were groaning, a few of the press contingency were obviously already bored after hearing only three words.

"For those of you who are unaware," Smyth carried on regardless. "I came up with this brainwave not long after I was appointed Superintendent. Why not look back, I thought. Why not look back over the past year and analyse how this year's performance compares to previous year's? And with that information, we can consider how we can improve for the following year. I know that everybody here is dying to hear how we've performed compared to this time last year, so without further ado I'll make a start."

"I need a drink," Bridge said to Yang Chu in the third row. "I swore last year that, next year I'd bring a hipflask of something, but I totally forgot again."

Superintendent Smyth spent the next hour and a half, informing the audience of how York Police had performed over the past year. The first thirty minutes were taken up explaining how his *complicated* points system worked. By the time he'd finished that, at least a quarter of the men and women sitting in front of him were asleep. In the second row from the back, the sound of loud snoring could be heard quite clearly.

When Smyth had finished offering his sincere thanks to everyone in attendance, most of the people there were still blissfully unaware that crime in York had risen over the past year. Nobody had really paid much attention and they didn't know that there had been more housebreaking and attempted robberies than ever before, and car theft had also increased. There had been fewer murders however than in the year prior, and in all but four of them, the perpetrators had been caught. And it was these four unsolved murders that every single representative of the press had come to hear about this evening.

"DS Smith," a woman in the front row said. "Are you any closer to apprehending this student killer?"

Smith moved closer to the microphone in front of him and thought hard about what he was going to say.

"We do have a suspect in custody. This suspect was arrested earlier today, and we are just waiting for forensics to confirm a few things."

"Do you have a name for us?" the woman pressed.

"I'm afraid not," Smith replied. "Like I said, we're waiting for forensics, and when they're finished, we'll be able to give you more."

"All the dead women were students," a man thrust his smart phone closer to where Smith was sitting. "Is this significant?"

"In what way?"

"You tell us. Is this suspect of yours linked to the University in any way?"

"No," Smith said. "This has nothing to do with York University."

"Detective," the first woman said. "Is it true that all of these women had their blood removed?"

Smith had been dreading this question. "That's right."

"Do you know why the killer did that?"

"I can't comment on that."

"Come on," the woman wasn't giving up so easily. "You must have some idea. Surely you can speculate as to the reason these young women were drained of blood?"

"Yes," Smith replied.

"Go on."

"You asked me if I could speculate as to the reason these young women were drained of blood," Smith said. "And I replied, yes. Yes, I can speculate, but as you're probably aware speculation doesn't solve crimes and I very much doubt that speculation makes for very convincing news."

There were a few titters of laughter in the audience.

"Does anybody have any more questions?" Smith was ready to wrap things up.

He felt like a drink.

"Detective Smith," a man who looked far too young to be a journalist said. "Gregory Freer, York student news blogger. I heard something on the campus grapevine about satanic rituals. Do you think these women had their blood removed to be used in some kind of pagan ceremony?"

"We have explored that line of enquiry," Smith really needed a drink now. "And we do not believe this was the reason these women were drained of blood."

"This suspect of yours," the student blogger said. "Can you at least tell us if it's a man or a woman?"

"Yes," Smith replied and if he'd been able to see the expression on DI Brownhill's face, he would have kept quiet. She looked horrified.

"Come on then," the blogger urged.

"It's a man or a woman," Smith said. "Now, if there are no more questions, I'm sure you have work to do. Thank you all for coming."

He switched off the microphone, stood up and left the conference room.

* * *

Smith took a long drink of his beer and closed his eyes. It had been a draining day and the pint of Theakston he was holding was just what the doctor ordered. He took the beer to the table where Bridge, Yang Chu and Brownhill were seated.

"Are you trying to send me into an early grave?" the DI asked when Smith sat down. "I almost had a heart attack back there. I thought you were about to tell them about Dr Dessai."

"I was just winding them up," Smith said. "I hate journalists. They're top three on my list of people I can't stand. Together with lawyers."

"What's the other one?" Yang Chu asked.

"Other what?"

"You said top three. Lawyers, journalists? What's the other one?"

"Students," Smith and Bridge said in unison.

"Why do you hate students so much?" Brownhill joined in. "Surely they're the future of the country?"

"Then God help us all," Smith downed the rest of his pint. "I don't know what happens to them in that first few months of University. They go in as normal kids who've finished school, and suddenly they mutate into horrible little bastards who think they can change the world."

"You've become rather cynical in your old age," Brownhill said with a wry smile on her face.

"World-weary more like it," Smith returned the smile. "Anyone for another drink? I'm buying."

"Where's Whitton?" Yang Chu asked when Smith returned with the drinks.

"At home with Laura," he replied. "She didn't feel like coming out. And I'd better make this my last one. At least we have another year before we have to endure another one of old Smyth's crime stat bollocks."

"Was anyone even paying attention?" Bridge asked. "I couldn't even tell you if crime was up or down from last year."

"Did you hear the snorer?" Yang Chu said. "That was hilarious. The Super didn't even notice."

"Smyth wouldn't have noticed if a herd of elephants came in and gate-crashed," Smith added.

He finished what was left in his glass and stood up. "I'll see you all bright and early tomorrow. Let's hope Webber and his team have something concrete for us tomorrow. I'd quite like to put this one behind me."

CHAPTER FIFTY

Smith had to drive under fifteen miles per hour the whole way to the station. A black frost had arrived in the night and the roads were treacherous. As he parked his car next to the station he realised he was the first of the team to arrive. The only other car was Baldwin's small blue Toyota. He made his way to the entrance of the station and almost slipped on a patch of black ice. Once inside, he headed straight up to the canteen. Baldwin was sitting on her own next to the coffee machine.

"Morning," Smith said. "Where is everyone? Did the clocks go back or something?"

"I think it's the weather," Baldwin suggested. "That ice is nasty, and it seems to slow everything down. Where's Whitton?"

"She'll be in soon. She's dropping Laura off at day-care."

Bridge walked in with Yang Chu. Bridge had a huge grin on his face, but Yang Chu seemed far from impressed.

"What's the joke?" Smith asked Bridge.

"Ask him," Bridge nudged Yang Chu on the shoulder. "He just saw his arse on a patch of ice outside in the car park. I wish I'd videoed it. It was bloody hilarious."

"Very funny," Yang Chu said. "I could have broken my back."

"You should have seen your face," Bridge wasn't giving up. "Priceless."

"What's the plan for today?" Yang Chu changed the subject.

"That depends on what forensics have for us," Smith said. "A lack of an alibi and a size five shoe won't wash with a jury – we need something concrete. Hopefully Webber will be able to tell us something later this morning."

He left the canteen and headed for his office. He switched on his PC and while he waited for it to boot up his eyes drifted to the photographs on his desk.

Two Lauras.

It suddenly struck him how alike they were. The photograph of his sister on the beach in Western Australia when she was eight years old, and the most recent one of his daughter were so similar Smith couldn't help smiling.

"My sister would have loved you," Smith spoke to the photograph of his daughter. "She would have spoilt you rotten."

"Who are you talking to?" Smith didn't realise his wife was standing in the doorway.

"I can't believe how much Laura looks like my sister," Smith told her. "It's uncanny."

Whitton came inside the office and took a closer look at the photographs.

"I still think Laura looks like you," she said. "Poor child. Have you seen the DI this morning?"

"Not yet. Her car is probably giving her trouble again. I wish Webber would give us something – I just want to put this investigation as far behind me as possible."

"You still don't think Dr Dessai is our killer, do you?"

"I didn't say that."

"Not in so many words," Whitton said. "But I know you. I know you have your doubts about her."

"It just doesn't feel right. I don't know what it is – I just get the feeling she's not the one."

Smith's phone started to ring. He took it out of his pocket, looked at the screen and smiled at Whitton.

"It's Webber," he told her. "Fingers crossed it's good news."

He pressed, *answer*. "Webber, what have you got?"

"Good news and bad news," the head of forensics told him. "Two of the paintings we took from Dr Dessai's house had traces of human blood on them. It's been confirmed. Not large quantities, but human blood, nevertheless. That's the good news."

"And the bad news?"

"Two things," Webber said. "Firstly, none of the shoes we took from the doctor's house matched the print in the carpet, and, secondly the blood on the two paintings didn't match the blood from any of the four victims."

"What about the painting sent to me for my birthday?"

"I didn't consider it a priority," Webber said. "I haven't had a look at it yet."

"It's a priority now," Smith said. "Check it out."

"I'll go over it later this morning. And you're welcome, by the way." Webber rang off first.

Smith put his phone down on the desk and sighed. "Dr Dessai isn't our killer. Which means we're back to square one. Again."

"You were right," Whitton said. "Again. At least that's one consolation."

"Some consolation. I suppose we just have to go back to the start. That's if Brownhill decides to show her face this morning."

Whitton's phone beeped to tell her she had a text message.

"That thing's been beeping all day and night recently," Smith commented. "Have you got a secret lover I don't know about?"

"Hardly," Whitton laughed. "It's Jessica. We've been chatting."

"Chatting with a bona fide nut-job? You've changed your tune."

"I like her," Whitton said. "She's different, but she's genuine. I think we could become good friends."

Smith shook his head and opened up his emails. There was nothing of any real importance.

"This just about sums things up," he pointed to the screen. "This sums up detective work perfectly. Waiting around for something to turn up. Well I can't be doing with it."

He stood up and left Whitton typing something on her phone.

CHAPTER FIFTY ONE

Two hours later and Brownhill still hadn't turned up. Smith had tried phoning her but the DI's phone went straight to voicemail.

"What does she think she's playing at?" Smith slammed his phone on the table in the canteen. "Has she forgotten we're in the middle of a bloody murder investigation?"

"Maybe she's convinced we have the murderer in custody," Yang Chu suggested. "Maybe she thinks it's all over."

"Then she hasn't spoken to her bloke," Smith was furious. "Webber has all but ruled Dr Dessai out."

He tried phoning Brownhill again with the same result.

"Fuck it," he said. "This is just great."

"What do you suggest we do?" Whitton asked.

"We can hold Dr Dessai for other twenty-four-hours, and then we've either got to charge her or let her go. Either decision will be made by Brownhill. Her disappearing act has left us twiddling our thumbs. And I'd prefer to twiddle my thumbs somewhere else. In the DI's absence, I'm assuming command, and I'm ordering myself to go home. The rest of you can do what the hell you want."

He stormed out the canteen leaving a group of wide-eyed detectives in his wake.

"He's in a good mood today," Bridge said.

"I don't know how you put up with him," Yang Chu said to Whitton.

"He takes things far too personally," Whitton defended her husband.

"Whatever," Bridge said. "I'm following suit. I'm going home to catch up on some well-needed sleep. You two might as well do the same."

"We can't just bugger off," Yang Chu said, ever conscientious.

"Why not?" Whitton said. "If Brownhill does decide to show her face, we're only a phone call away. I'm going to see a soon to be good friend."

Yang Chu sat staring out the window for a while. He was unsure of what to do. It took him all of a minute to follow the example of his colleagues and go home.

Smith shut down his computer and picked up his coat. He put it on and was about to leave the office when his phone started to ring.

"About bloody time," he said, assuming it was Brownhill.

"Smith," it was Grant Webber. "I've got something."

"I'm listening," Smith said and held his breath.

"That painting someone sent you for your birthday," Webber continued. "It was painted in human blood. The whole thing was painted in blood."

"I knew it," Smith's stomach was getting warmer.

"I compared it to the blood of the dead women, and I came up with two matches. The blood used on the painting came from both Taylor Fox and Rene Downs."

"So, the killer sent me the painting," Smith said. "Why would they do that?"

"There's more," Webber said. "And this is the scary part. There was what looked like a partial print on the painting. It was smudged but it was enough. It's a thumb print, and more than that, the owner of the thumb that made the print is on our database."

"Dr Dessai?" Smith said.

"No," Webber paused for a moment. "The person who painted that picture is Jessica Blakemore."

Smith was out of the office in seconds. He ran down the corridor, bumping into Yang Chu by the front desk.

"Where are Whitton and Bridge?" he shouted.

"Bridge went home, and Whitton said something about seeing a soon to be good friend. Whatever she meant by that."

"Fuck," Smith said. "Get hold of Bridge and tell him to get to this address straight away. Jessica Blakemore is our killer."

He gave him her address and took out his phone. He brought up Whitton's number and pressed call. The all too familiar 'The person you have dialled is not available at present,' was all he got.

"Bridge is on his way there," Yang Chu told him.

"You come with me," Smith said.

"We'll go in my car," Yang Chu suggested. "It's a lot quicker than yours."

CHAPTER FIFTY TWO

The artist gazed at the pool of blood that had settled on the floor in the kitchen.

No two person's blood is alike, she decided. In colour, texture or smell, each of us has unique blood.

This blood was richer in colour than the last batch. This one would help to produce the most exquisite landscape. The detective's eyes were open, but she couldn't see anything. Her face had turned pale and was already cold to the touch. The artist looked into her eyes and closed them. Now she could sleep.

The sound of the doorbell rang throughout the house and the artist flinched. Then she smiled.

"It's time," she said. "Time to go home."

CHAPTER FIFTY THREE

Smith was out of the car before Yang Chu had even stopped. Whitton's car was parked outside Jessica Blakemore's house. Bridge's car was parked behind it.

"No," he screamed and ran up the path. "No."

He opened the front door and came face to face with Bridge. The detective sergeant's face was deathly pale.

"Don't go in there, Smith," he warned. "Don't go in there."

Smith tried to get past, but Bridge blocked his path.

"She's dead, Smith. She's gone."

Smith shoved him so hard that Bridge struggled to stay on his feet. He teetered to one side and regained his balance. He followed Smith into the kitchen.

Detective Inspector Bryony Brownhill was sitting on a chair in the middle of the room. Her face had turned a bluish-grey colour and her eyes were closed. A pool of blood lay on the tiles beneath her. A thin film had formed on the surface. Whitton was sitting on the floor against the back door. A whimpering Jessica Blakemore sat next to her. Her hands were handcuffed behind her back and she was muttering something about going home.

Smith scooped Whitton up into his arms and pulled her away from the whimpering woman. He helped her out of the kitchen, and they stood in the hallway, arms tight around each other. Neither of them spoke. Yang Chu came in and stood staring, eyes wide open. He walked past them into the kitchen.

"I thought it was you," Smith said at last and the first tears came. "I thought it was you she'd killed. I can't lose you, Erica. I thought it was you."

The sound of sirens could be heard outside. Two police cars and an ambulance arrived at the same time. Smith and Whitton walked past two uniformed officers into the street. Arm in arm they walked away from Jessica Blakemore's house.

CHAPTER FIFTY FOUR

Bryony Brownhill was buried ten days later. The funeral was a modest affair with only family and close friends in attendance. Her phone records showed she'd received a phone call from Jessica Blakemore the morning she was killed. What was spoken about in that phone call is still a mystery, but Brownhill was somehow lured to her death. The autopsy report showed she had just ten percent of her blood left in her system. It also showed to everyone's horror that she had no traces of any drugs in her system – she was simply overpowered by Jessica Blakemore and tied to a chair. She was very much aware of what was happening to her when her blood was being drained.

Jessica Blakemore never did go *home*. She spoke quite candidly of her reasons for killing all those women. She longed to be back inside the tranquil confines of the psychiatric hospital. The killing had been a means to an end. But the secure facility she ended up in was a far cry from the caring and free environment of the hospital where she'd spent five years of her life.

* * *

"She caught the ball," Smith came inside to tell Whitton.
Laura had been practicing and this was the first time she'd managed to place her tiny hands around the tennis ball and not drop it.
"She's going to be a top cricket player someday."
Whitton wasn't listening. She was staring out of the window into the back garden.
"Are you alright?" Smith asked her.
"Chalmers just phoned," Whitton said. "He phoned about Jessica Blakemore."
"What about her?"

"She's dead," Whitton turned to face her husband. "Chalmers thought you'd want to know. She was found in her room with her throat slashed. She was holding a piece of broken glass in her hand. It looks like she killed herself."

Smith's eyes narrowed and he gazed out of the window at his daughter. She was throwing the tennis ball in the air. This time she dropped it.

"It was probably inevitable," he said. "Come outside. Laura wants to show you how she catches a ball."

THE END

Printed in Great
Britain
by Amazon